Murder in the Catskills

A MURDER AND A MYSTERY —
WITH A BIT OF HISTORY

NORMAN J. VAN VALKENBURGH

MURDER
IN THE
CATSKILLS

PURPLE MOUNTAIN PRESS
Fleischmanns, New York

First Edition, 1992

published by
PURPLE MOUNTAIN PRESS, LTD.
Main Street, P.O. Box E3
Fleischmanns, New York 12430-0378
914-254-4062

Copyright © 1992 by Norman J. Van Valkenburgh

Library of Congress Cataloging-In-Publication Data

Van Valkenburgh, Norman J. (Norman James), 1930-
    Murder in the Catskills / Norman J. Van Valkenburgh. — 1st ed.
        p.   cm.
    ISBN 0-935796-37-1 (pbk.)
    1. Catskill Mountains Region (N.Y.)—Fiction. I. Title.
    PS3572.A5445M86   1992
    813'.54—dc20   92-41885
                                             CIP

Manufactured in the United States of America

My wife, that Dot Cross of my youth, shares the past and the passing years with me. She is an inveterate reader of murder mysteries set in the English countryside; although she will not find the locale here to fit that mold, she will recognize it nonetheless.

This one's for her.

Table of Contents

Prologue

THE STONE WALL WAS AN OLD ONE, probably built in the early 1800s by the first settlers in the valley, he thought. It had tumbled over in places and was covered by fallen tree limbs here and there. It wouldn't do a very good job of keeping the cows in the pasture — if any cows were here, which they weren't. Neither were the pastures good for much else than growing brush now. Cows had given way when the city folks found the valley and thought it would be a good place to spend the summers. Some point to that, he thought. If he lived in the city, he sure as hell would look for some cooler spot to spend those hot and humid days. But for one who lived in the country like he had all his life, he resented the invasion of the city people and the changes they were bringing to the Mountain Top and its culture. Why couldn't they have found that cooler spot someplace else?

The other side of that issue was the city people needed a survey when they bought a piece of land and that kept him busy in his old age. At least it seemed like old age sometimes, especially like today when the direct sun of early July beat down on his head. The stream was dry, he was thristy and worse, he had forgotten to bring his matches so he couldn't even light his pipe. Also, the slope of the mountain seemed much steeper than when he first had climbed it some forty years ago.

He knew what he'd find when he got to the far corner — there would be the pile of stones he had built back then. Rebuilt was better term; he had found the small pile of stones set in 1810 as a line marker by the original surveyor, John Wigram. No one else had ever recognized it for what it was, so he had added a great lot of bigger stones to it so that the surveyors who followed him couldn't mistake it for anything other than the property corner. Probably no other surveyor would ever come all the way up here anyway. Seemed to him the modern-day surveyors were all looking for flatland work—if they couldn't drive to every corner of a property, they didn't want to survey it.

That old pile of stones had had character though and he had hated to destroy it by piling more stones on it. The stone wall had character too as most old stone walls did. He always admired them and the craftsmen who had built them. They weren't really craftsmen though; they were farmers as all the first settlers hereabouts had been. The land was so covered with stones it had to be cleared off, so that grass could grow and the livestock could find pasture. The farmers took the stones and, in order to get them out of the way, piled them in long, straight lines that came down off one mountain, crossed the creek bottom, and headed up the next mountain. They followed patent, great lot, and tract lines that had been laid out by Wigram, the Woosters, the Cockburns and the other early land surveyors. Other walls ran randomly about following creek banks, tops of ridges, and other natural features. These were lot lines too, between the sheep lot and the cow lot, he chuckled to himself.

He cursed as a branch of a thorn apple hooked into his hat and lifted it from his head. If only the Catskill Mountain farmers had been able to find a market for rock and thorn apple, they'd be millionaires. But they couldn't so they had remained poor. That is, until the city folks showed up and paid them three and four times what the land was worth just so they could have some spot of earth to call their own and where they could build a log cabin and rough it each summer. Rough it, hell, he thought, rough was back when those guys who built the wall were here. Things would never be the same as they were then; he had resigned himself to that. At least the walls would be. And the thorn apples too—the city people would never be able to get rid of those.

The slope of the mountain became steeper the farther he went. The stone wall ended at the base of a small ledge of rocks—the high cliffs were on up the mountain. He climbed the ledge, took out his hand compass and sighted back down the wall. Once he had the bearing of it set, he turned around, sighted up the slope on the reverse bearing and picked out a large maple nearly on line beyond the next ledge. When he reached it, he saw, just as he suspected, it had been blazed for line by a surveyor of long-ago. The map of his survey of forty years before noted this line as being marked with old blazes. He still expected to find a few of the larger trees to have those older marks. He didn't suppose the young surveyors even knew what an old blaze looked like. Well! no need to irritate himself with all that again.

He kept climbing, following the line of his compass bearing, occasionally correcting to an old mark. These were few and far between now. He found one old hemlock, rotten and decaying, laying on the ground near where his bearing ran. However, enough of the bark of it remained so that he was still able to see the old blaze. Marks on hemlock trees were easy to pick out if you knew what to look for; however, not that many hemlocks had survived the tanning business that stripped the mountains in the early 1800s. How this one had escaped was a good question.

As he got nearer the high ledge, the angle of the slope increased significantly. In the winter, with the ground here covered with snow, it would have been difficult to continue, especially if the cliffs above were coated with ice. Any melt water from them would have run down the mountain and been refrozen to coat the slope with a slippery surface.

The high ledge or cliff, as it ringed the mountain, could be seen from down in the valley. It literally cut the Ford lands and those adjoining on each side into two parts with that above the ledge being inaccessible except on foot. That is, if the one on foot could climb the ledge, which was what he was wondering as he approached it.

The compass bearing brought him to the base of one of the sheerest faces of the ledge. Obviously, he would find no way up there. He turned left and walked along the bottom of the ledge into the Ford property. Here and there, breaks split the face of the cliff, but didn't offer a practical way up. Finally, he reached a wide rift where a number of maple saplings provided enough hand holds so that he was able to clamber to the top. In his younger days, he would have tried one of the narrow crevasses, but now, in his sixties, the easier way made more sense.

He worked his way west back to the point above where the compass bearing had hit the base of the cliff and continued following the bearing up the mountain. The angle eased off a bit now and he made better time. Soon he saw the large pile of stones he had built at the site of the smaller pile of stones that had originally been set as a line marker. It had been a long time; he had found, built and rebuilt a lot of corners since then. This had been one of the first that others before him had passed by, not recognizing the few scattered stones for what they meant. Now it was obvious to all who came here and was made more so by the yellow paint that was daubbed on the stones and on the witness marks hacked into the trees circling the corner. The land up the mountain was owned by the State now. The yellow paint went both to the right and to the left of the corner highlighting the blazes on the trees that delineated the boundary between the State land to the south and the Ford and the other private properties to the north.

That had been the reason for the survey back in the 1920s. He was then in his first years of working for the State and had been sent to survey the upper part of the old Musgrave property that was being purchased by the State for addition to the Catskill Forest Preserve. Following the survey and the purchase, it was up to the local Forest Ranger to periodically walk the line, clear out the brush from it, and repaint the blazes every ten years or so. Obviously Roger Hurley, the present Ranger, was doing his job. The yellow paint looked recent, no more than two years old.

3

He sat down on a flat rock beside the pile of stones. It had been a long, hard climb — he was over two-thirds of the way up the mountain. The spring was higher still, up in the State land, but he knew where it was. The use of the spring by the Ford property had been an exception from the State purchase and he had located it during the early survey. He would have to locate it again for the split of the Ford lands, but that could wait until he did the actual survey a couple of weeks from now.

He could see the flat land of the valley far below and the South Branch stream winding its way westerly. The small hamlet of the same name was clustered at the big sweeping bend in the stream where it turned and flowed north heading for the New York City reservoir some ten miles away. He really wished now he had remembered his matches, a smoke of his pipe would be a pleasant way to spend the next half hour or so. The back of his shirt was soaked through and the sweat ran down his face from under the brim of his hat. Probably too hot for a smoke anyway, he consoled himself. Instead, he munched on the apple he had brought along in the small rucksack he always carried when he planned to be in the woods for more than a couple of hours. He'd have to remember to fill the waterproof match box in the side pocket of it when he got home that night.

The apple gone, he started down the mountain, but headed more to the east as he went. The Fords wanted the property to be split into two equal parts with the dividing line to run through the so-called "big rock" on top of the high ledge. Big rock, hell, it was monolithic. It had always been a curiosity hereabouts, perched as it was on the very brink of the cliff; so close, the story went, that it teetered back and forth when a high wind blew straight up the mountain. He had never heard of anyone being there during a high wind and he didn't put much stock in most tales told by the old-timers anyway.

Still, the big rock was an odd thing. It had, sometime long ago, slid for some distance down the mountain. That could be seen by the long, deep gully that defined the track of its slide. It reached at least 200 feet up the slope and ran down straight as an arrow to the back side of the rock. Other nearby large rocks rested at the lower end of similar tracks, but none were as deep or as long as that marking the slide of the big rock. The explanation was that a heavy, prolonged rain in that time past had turned the soil of the upper slopes of the mountain into a liquid mud that had run under the rocks to loosen them. Gravity had then started the slide. Why the big rock had stopped at the edge of the cliff and had not gone over was not so easily explained.

It was, indeed, big. It was nearly thirty feet high and well over thirty feet broad so as to be some one hundred feet in circumference. The sides of it were sheer with no route to the flat top of the rock, except on the downhill side where the force of the north wind had eroded it away into an uneven surface. Some young lad from the village, who fancied himself a climber, had tried to scale the ledge and the rock some twenty-five years ago. He had reached the top of the ledge, said his friend, who watched from below, but in reaching for a hold on the rock, he slipped and fell to the scree below breaking his neck on impact. After that, the Fords posted their entire property, and ringed the area of the ledge and the big rock with signs particularly warning of the danger and admonishing all to keep out. As far as he knew, no one had ever climbed to the top of the big rock.

He saw it through the trees from some distance away; it was too big to miss from any direction. As he approached it, he was surprised to see that a large maple tree, on the uphill side, had been uprooted, probably in that high wind of last spring, and leaned at a 45-degree angle against the rock. It presented a perfect bridge from the ground to the top. Still having some adventure in his soul after all these years, he decided to have a go at it and leave his name to history as the first person to reach the top of "big rock."

The climb up onto the broad trunk of the fallen tree was an easy scramble with the now bare roots providing sufficient handholds. He balanced his way along the first fifteen feet or so of the trunk to the first round of limbs. He cut his way through for the next twenty-five feet with the double-bitted cruiser's ax he always carried, leaving enough limbs to hold onto as he went on up the tree. Once, heights didn't bother him, but in the last few years he found that the closer to the ground he stayed, the more comfortable he felt. As he neared the top, he didn't look down the thirty feet or so to the ground and hoped the rock didn't start teetering now.

He was glad to reach the top and pushed his way through the last few limbs without pausing to cut them off. He was glad he hadn't, because he needed them to hold onto in order to steady himself from the shock of what he saw. He wasn't the first one to climb "big rock" after all. There, near the upper edge of the flat top of it, lay a skeleton. It was bleached from the weather, but it was, unquestionably, a human skeleton.

April 20, 1708

ANNE by the Grace of God of England Scotland France & Ireland Queen Defendr of the faith &c To all to whom these p^{r}sents may in any wise Concerne Sendeth Greeting WHEREAS our Loving Subjects Johannes Hardenbergh, Leonard Lewis, Phillip Rokeby, William Nottingham, Benjamin Faneuil, Peter Fauconnier, & Robt Lurting by their humbly Petition Presented unto our Right Trusty and well beloved Couzin Edwd. Viscount Cornbury Capt. Genll. & Govr. in Chiefe in & over our Province of New Yorke & Territories thereon Depending in America and Vice Admirall of the same &c In Councill Have Pray'd our Grant & Confirmation of a Certain Tract of Vacant and unappropriated Land Scituate in the Countys of Ulster & Albany beginning att the Sand Bergh or Hills att ye Northeast Corner of the Lands Granted to Ebenezer Willson, Derick Van den burgh &c att Minisinck so Running all along their Line Northwesterly as the said Line Runs to the ffish Kill or River and so to the head thereof Including the same thence on a Direct Line to the head of a Certain Small River Commonly Known by the Name of Cartwright's kill and so by the Northerly Side of the said Kill or River to the Northermost Bounds of Kingstown on the said Kill or River thence by the Bounds of Kingstown Hurley Marbletown Rochester and other Patented Lands to the Southward thereof to the said Sand Bergh the place where it first begun the which Petition wee being minded to Grant Know Yee that of our Especiall Grace Certain knowledge and meer motion wee have Given Granted Ratifyed and Confirmed and in and by these Presents for ourselves our Heires and Successors Doe Give Grant Ratifye & Confirme unto the said Johannes Hardenbergh Leonard Lewis Phillip Rokeby William Nottingham Benjamin Faneuil Peter Fauconnier and Robert Lurting all and Singular the Tract of Land and Premises above mentioned . . . .

Chapter 1

The Hardenburgh Patent

FOR THE TWO HUNDRED YEARS following Henry Hudson's first sighting of the Catskills (or the Blew Hills, as they were called by his mate, Robert Juet) from the deck of the Halve Maen in September of 1609, little interest was taken in them. The settlers on the banks of the Hudson River and the level land reaching from the west shore of the river to the foot of these mountains looked upon the Great Wall of Manitou, the eastern escarpment of the Catskills, as a barrier and knew the land behind it was rough and unfit for farming. From these rugged and forbidding mountains came tales of ferocious wild animals, renegade Indians, and ghostly apparitions and the settlers were filled with terror when they considered going into these high hills. The mountains remained a remote wilderness as the Dutch, who had settled the flat lands, neither dared nor wanted to venture into their deep cloves or climb the steep ridges of their mysterious peaks shrouded with dense and dark groves of hemlocks.

By the late 1600s, almost all of the land surrounding the Catskills had been patented by the Crown. These early grants included the Kingston Commons, the Marbletown Comons, the Hurley Patent, the Rochester Patent, and the Catskill Patent. In all, forty-two grants, ranging in size from a few hundred acres to fifty or sixty thousand acres, parceled out the lands around the Catskills prior to the Revolutionary War.

The largest Colonial grant was the Hardenburgh Patent and the full story of how Johannis Hardenbergh "and his Company" were able to lay their hands on the 1.5-million acres of the so-called Great Patent is a difficult one to pin down. One story goes that Hardenbergh fought valiently at the Battle of Blenheim in the War of the Spanish Succession and the grateful Anne "by the Grace of God of England Scotland France & Ireland, Queen

Defendr of the faith" knighted him and further expressed her gratitude by granting him all (or nearly all) of "the great mountain commonly called the Blew Hills." The record indicates otherwise — at the time of Blenheim, Hardenbergh was in Kingston running his store, trading with the Indians for furs and with the Dutch farmers for wheat.

The store was not Hardenbergh's in the beginning. It was owned by his father-in-law, one Jacob Rusten, who turned it over to him in 1700, a year or so after Hardenbergh had married Catherine Rusten. Jacob Rusten was one of the landed gentry and owned much of what later became known as the Kingston Flats, that fertile outwash of the Rondout and Esopus creeks. In addition to following his father-in-law in the trading business, Hardenbergh, like Rusten, acquired property through the process of petitioning the Governor of New York for grants of small tracts of wilderness land at the foot of the Blew Hills and, then, converting it into farmland.

While the Blew Hills or Catskills were craggy and remote, Hardenbergh and Rusten realized the value of the land in the valleys that lay between the steep ridges. Others did, too. In 1704, a group of farmers, having outgrown their farms along the Esopus Creek, petitioned the Governor for some of these valleys — to pasture their cattle, so they said.

While no profile or biography of Johannis Hardenbergh has ever been discovered, it is possible to draw a picture of him and to determine some of the milestones in his life from other records. In 1690, at the young age of twenty, he was appointed sheriff of Ulster County by the then Acting Governor, Jacob Leisler, whose devout followers included Rusten and Hardenburgh's brother-in-law, Leonard Lewis, an alderman of New York City. However, this term as sheriff was short-lived — Leisler was hanged as a traitor soon after Hardenbergh's appointment. In 1710, with a new governor sympathetic to the views held by the earlier Leisler supporters, Hardenbergh regained his old office.

One of the Hardenbergh's responsibilities as sheriff was serving as justice of the peace. The record lists him as Major Johannis Hardenbergh, Esq., High Sherriffee, with the Major coming from his involvement in the militia, which was only just enough to gain the military appellation. Most of his later life was spent in trying to straighten out the boundaries of and title to the Great Patent for these were, indeed, a tangled skein.

In making Colonial grants, it was the rule of the English to require the Indian title to be first extinguished. It was customary to apply to the Governor and the Council of the Colonial government for leave to purchase. If the petition was granted, a treaty was held with the Indian tribe asserting ownership of the land involved, and a deed was obtained. A warrant was then issued to the Surveyor General for a survey, and field notes and a map were reported. On completion of the survey, the Attorney General was directed to prepare a draft of the patent, which was submitted to the Governor and the Council. If approved, the patent was engrossed upon parchment, sealed and issued. The fees incident to procuring a patent were important sources of income to the officers and other government officials concerned.

At the time of the grant of the Hardenburgh Patent, no rule or other requirement set a limit on the amount of acreage that could fall to the share of an individual patentee. However, it was the custom, generally adhered to by the various governors of New York, that the size should not exceed 2,000 acres per person. This limitation was formalized in instructions from the Lords of Trade in the same year (1708) as the granting of the Hardenburgh Patent and was reduced to 1,000 acres per person by provisions adopted in 1753. Whatever the authority of the limitation, it was evaded by associating great numbers of nominal associates, figureheads, and dummies as parties to the original petition. The officers through whose hands the papers of the patents passed were also often largely interested in them. The colonial government, in this respect, became exceedingly corrupt and the granting of the Hardenburgh Patent stands as a good example of this corruption.

With the custom being 2,000 acres as the limit that could be granted to an individual, how could seven men arrange for a patent of a single land parcel larger than the State of Rhode Island? Certainly it must have been misrepresented as to its size. Some indications suggest the Colonial Governor was promised a share. Record proof exists that the Surveyor General came in for a share equal to that of the seven patentees. Some strange doings were involved in the process with perhaps the strangest being the Governor, who bestowed upon himself the title, His High Mightiness.

Edward Hyde, Viscount Cornbury, was a nephew (by marriage) of James II. However, that didn't prevent Cornbury from deserting the King and leading his regiment of cavalry to William of Orange when William invaded England in 1689. The grateful William appointed Cornbury governor of New York and, when Anne became Queen on William's death, she continued the tenure of her cousin, the Viscount. While Cornbury had a number of quirks that didn't endear him to New Yorkers, the oddest was his habit, at the same hour each day, of dressing himself in the finest of silk and lace of ladies' fashion and strolling along the ramparts of Fort Anne waving his fan at the soldiers below. That strange behavior was, at least, seen by only a few. However, Cornbury took his fan to the opening of the New York Assembly in 1702. When asked why he performed that duty in a hooped gown and headdress, he stated he was representing Queen Anne, "and in all respect I ought to represent her as faithfully as I can."

Cornbury aligned himself with the rich and openingly opposed those of rival factions and parties, especially those who had been supporters of Governor Jacob Leisler. If Hardenbergh, one of the most staunch of the

Leisler Party, had any hopes of obtaining a large grant of land, they were dashed when Cornbury arrived in New York. But, perhaps more than any other governor, Cornbury looked upon land and the granting of it as a means of lining his own pockets and overcoming his lack of personal fortune. Notwithstanding, Hardenbergh was only one man. He couldn't, by himself, petition for the flat lands in the Blew Hills and he needed to do something quickly before a grant was finalized to the Esopus farmers. With the help of his father-in-law, Hardenbergh gathered together six other men (or was it seven?), who became known, in time, as "his Company."

William Nottingham was a justice of the peace from Marbletown and later served as witness to at least one of the deeds whereby the Indians sold to Rusten and Hardenbergh. His only other qualification was his availability — he was Rusten's son-in-law and, thus, Hardenbergh's brother-in-law.

Leonard Lewis was an early settler of Poughkeepsie, across the Hudson River, and was another of Hardenbergh's brothers-in-law, having married Hardenbergh's oldest sister, Elisabeth. Lewis was, at one time or another, a member of the Colonial Assembly, a Colonel in the militia, an Alderman in New York City, and a Judge in the Dutchess County Court of Common Pleas. He was well-known in the halls of power and was a friend of many along the way.

Benjamin Faneuil was a trader and distiller of rum in New York City. He was a Huguenot and his brother, Andrew, was a merchant in Boston. It was one of Benjamin's sons, Peter, who, after inheriting his uncle's fortune, built Faneuil Hall and later donated it to the people of Boston. It is not clear how Faneuil came to be one of the "Company," but indications are he was brought in by Lewis.

Peter Fauconnier, who was generally listed only as "Gentleman," was also a Huguenot, a merchant, and a cohort of Viscount Cornbury's from their army days. When Cornbury was appointed Governor, he named Fauconnier as one of his closest advisors. In that position, Fauconnier served as intermediary between Cornbury and the pirates. He was Commissioner of Revenue, Receiver General, and Naval Officer of the Port of New York. It was through him that Cornbury was able to pillage the public treasury. Not surprisingly, a statement of Cornbury's describes Fauconnier as "a very honest man." It appears that Fauconnier guided the Great Patent through its various windings and turnings from the original petition to the final grant.

Philip Rokeby was a surgeon and the son-in-law of New York's mayor (from 1707 to 1710), Ebenezer Willson, who was a principal in the Minisink Patent, which adjoined on the south the land being petitioned for by Hardenbergh and "his Company." Rokeby was another confidant of Cornbury's. However, he was only a stand-in for Major Bickley, the acting Attorney General of New York. Bickley served as legal advisor to both the petitioners and, in his position as Attorney General, the Crown. It appears that Bickley drew all the legal papers necessary to the Patent for whomever needed them.

Robert Lurting was another front man. Lurting had, for many years, been Mayor of New York City and was involved with the pirates who frequented the harbors of that city. Lurting would show up again in 1711 as one of three commissioners appointed to partition the lands of the Minisink Patent among its twenty-three proprietors. However, in the case of the Hardenburgh Patent, he was acting for Thomas Wenham, a member of the Governor's Council. Wenham was a sea captain and merchant in New York City. At various times before being appointed to the Governor's Council, he was Commissioner of Customs, an Assemblyman, a Judge of the Colonial Court, and an Alderman of New York City. He made a great point of his position as warden of Trinity Church (a position also held by Lurting). He also had connections with the pirates and one of the most notorious of them devised "to my beloved friend, Mr. Thomas Wenham, my negro wench called Shoutone." Wenham, Rokeby, and Fauconnier were among the twenty-three patentees of the large (one hundred and seventy square miles) Minisink Patent adjoining the Hardenburgh Patent on the south.

With the use of two dummies being known (each of them declared publicly that he was standing in for another), it has been speculated that one of the others, probably Peter Fauconnier, was standing in for Cornbury, but this has never been proven nor has any conveyance of an interest in the Patent held by Cornbury ever been found.

So it was that the petitioners for The Great Hardenburgh Patent turned out to be a bunch of in-laws and outlaws at the head of the Colonial government. If, however, Hardenbergh and his six fellow petitioners made up the total of "the Company," how come they each voted themselves only a one-eighth share in the Patent? The answer is that the seven, long before the Patent was granted, conveyed an equal share of it to the Surveyor General, Augustine Graham. Because of his office, Graham was specifically forbidden from being granted land. He couldn't even risk having a dummy, but by a clever method called lease and release, each of the other seven conveyed Graham an equal or one-eighth interest.

Why the largess? Certainly none of "the Company" was noted for his generosity. And Graham was not one to endear himself to others—one source says he was known for rousing his neighbors in New York City "at night by breaking windows in fits of alcoholic exuberance." The answer goes back to that 1704 petition by the Esopus farmers for the additional land they needed as pasture for their livestock. Their petition said they were "informed that between the north bounds of Kingston and the great mountain commonly called the Blew Hills there is found vacant Land left unappropriated fitt for Commonage [pasture] and firewood but not for cultiva-

11

tion. But your Petitioners cannot describe unto your Excellency the exact bounds and limits thereof." So, Governor Cornbury and his Council ordered the Surveyor General to make a survey to determine these "exact bounds and limits."

Cornbury and the Council received the petition of the Esopus farmers on October 4, 1704, and promptly authorized the survey. However, this survey turned out to be one of those that never gets done—Surveyor General Graham, usually efficient in carrying out his duties, seemed not able to get this one under way. In the meantime, Hardenbergh and "his Company" were moving much more swiftly. Rusten was dickering with the Indians attempting to purchase their rights; Bickley was preparing legal documents (and signing them too, it seems, because the spelling of Johannis Hardenbergh's name in signature differed from document to document); Fauconnier was seeing that the right papers got to the right place (and the wrong ones to the wrong place).

At the July 1706 meeting of Cornbury and his Council, the petition of Hardenbergh (spelled therein as Hardenbrough) and Company was received saying they had "Discovered a small Tract vacant and unappropriated Land In the County of Ulster and Disining [desiring] to settle and Improve the same if your Excellency bee pleasd to favor him and his Company therein." Even though the petition did not describe the land, a "Licence [was] Issued accordingly" and no survey was ordered. By the end of July, Rusten had a deed from the Indians—the fact that it was from the wrong Indian tribe and didn't cover the same lands as in the petition didn't seem to matter.

In October of 1706, Graham was finally able to accomplish the survey for the Esopus farmers. Then, however, he experienced some problems in completing the map. That wasn't finished and presented to the Governor and the Council until June of 1707. The farmers realized by then a rival petition was in the field and began an action requiring priority to be given to their petition. It was too late for that to have any effect, but neither did the farmers realize or reckon with the power "the Company" represented.

But "the Company" itself was then in danger of losing out. It was fast becoming obvious that Cornbury had not long to sit in the Governor's chair. Word of his mishandling of government affairs and his eccentricities had been reaching England for some time and word drifted back that Queen Anne and the Lords of Trade had had enough. On March 18, 1708, the final petition of Hardenbergh and "his Company" was approved. On March 28, 1708, the ax fell—Queen Anne removed Cornbury from office with the effective date to be when the newly-appointed governor arrived in New York. Atlantic crossings were slow in those days and long before the ship carrying the new governor reached harbor, the Patent was issued on April 20, 1708.

The Hardenburgh Patent is the largest of the colonial grants in New York State. The boundaries of it extend from the Pennsylvania line at Narrowsburg to Lake Utsayantha above Stamford, and from the West Branch of the Delaware River to within five miles of the Hudson River at its northeasterly corner. It covers much of four counties; Delaware, Greene, Sullivan, and Ulster; and a small part of a fifth — Schoharie.

If any grant or patent ever violated the customs, rules, and laws of the time, it was the Hardenburgh Patent. Its total size of 1.5-million acres, of course, exceeded the limit of 16,000 acres that should have been granted to the eight patentees. No survey was completed prior to the grant so the land could be accurately described. And the patentees did not acquire the Indian title before the grant was finalized. In fact, it was not until nearly forty years later that deeds were acquired from the Indians — the Patent was so large, it was necessary to obtain title from two different tribes.

The deed from the Esopus Indians is dated June 6, 1746, and covers the northerly part of the Patent. The deed from the Minisink Indians is dated August 2, 1746, and covers the southerly part of the Patent. The Esopus Indians received one hundred seventy-five pounds for their land and the Minisink Indians received one hundred twenty-five pounds. The total of three hundred pounds amounted to about $700.00 for the 1.5 million acres, or about 2,150 acres for each dollar.

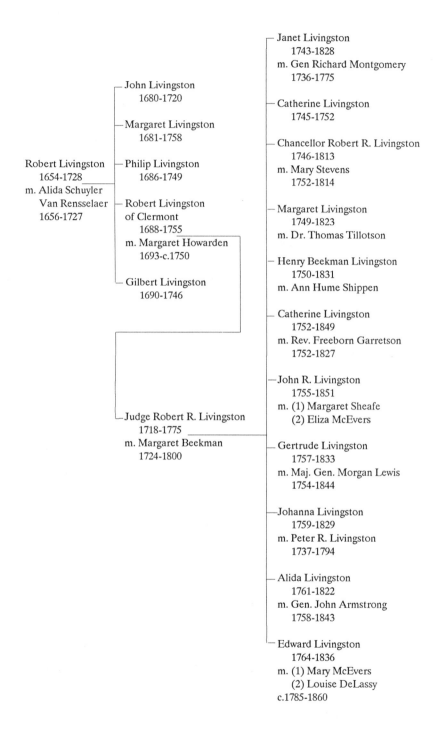

Robert Livingston
1654-1728
m. Alida Schuyler
Van Rensselaer
1656-1727

— John Livingston
1680-1720

— Margaret Livingston
1681-1758

— Philip Livingston
1686-1749

— Robert Livingston
of Clermont
1688-1755
m. Margaret Howarden
1693-c.1750

— Gilbert Livingston
1690-1746

— Judge Robert R. Livingston
1718-1775
m. Margaret Beekman
1724-1800

— Janet Livingston
1743-1828
m. Gen Richard Montgomery
1736-1775

— Catherine Livingston
1745-1752

— Chancellor Robert R. Livingston
1746-1813
m. Mary Stevens
1752-1814

— Margaret Livingston
1749-1823
m. Dr. Thomas Tillotson

— Henry Beekman Livingston
1750-1831
m. Ann Hume Shippen

— Catherine Livingston
1752-1849
m. Rev. Freeborn Garretson
1752-1827

—John R. Livingston
1755-1851
m. (1) Margaret Sheafe
(2) Eliza McEvers

— Gertrude Livingston
1757-1833
m. Maj. Gen. Morgan Lewis
1754-1844

—Johanna Livingston
1759-1829
m. Peter R. Livingston
1737-1794

— Alida Livingston
1761-1822
m. Gen. John Armstrong
1758-1843

— Edward Livingston
1764-1836
m. (1) Mary McEvers
(2) Louise DeLassy
c.1785-1860

14

Chapter 2

The Livingstons

BY THE TIME OF THE INDIAN DEEDS, a number of the original patentees had passed on. The title to their shares had devolved to others and a new power was emerging to wheel and deal the Patent.

Leonard Lewis had died and left his share divided among his twelve children. (Some sources say eleven. The later deed of partition lists twelve names without saying how many were children of Lewis. However, when a 1790 survey divided the Lewis land, eleven shares were laid out.) Benjamin Faneuil died in 1719 and, while he left his "Indian boy Peter and my silver watch" to his oldest son, he devised all his real property to "my beloved consort Anne during her widowhood."

Soon after the grant of the Great Patent, Philip Rokeby conveyed his interest to the man for whom he served as dummy, Attorney General Major Bickley. Bickley died in 1724 and left "my whole estate, both real and personal, lands, heridaments, goods and chattels whatsoever to my loving wife, Elizabeth." In 1741, Elizabeth Bickley conveyed her one-eighth share in the Patent to Robert Livingston.

William Nottingham had also died and his heirs sold their one- eighth interest to Robert Livingston and Gulian Verplanck. Peter Fauconnier was still alive and sold his one-eighth share directly to Livingston and Verplanck.

Augustine Graham died in 1719 and ten years later the other seven interests conveyed a one-eighth share to his son, James Graham, to confirm the complicated and confusing leases and releases that had been transferred to the Surveyor General prior to the grant. The deed of September 6, 1729, states that "Augustine Graham Esquire late Surveyor General of the Province of New York tho not named in the Said Letters Patent was nevertheless Verily and indead equally Concerned in the Right and proprietie of the Said Lands given and granted by the said Letters Patent and is entitled to one Eighth Part of all the Said Tract of Land." In 1741, James Graham sold his one-eighth share to Livingston and Verplanck.

Robert Lurting conveyed his one-eighth share to Thomas Wenham, for whom he had acted as dummy, soon after the Patent was granted. Wenham conveyed his interest to his son, John. John Wenham, who lived in London, held onto that interest until 1751, when he sold it to a group of eight individuals, including Robert Livingston. Johannis Hardenbergh died in 1748; however, in 1743, he had, through power of attorney, conveyed his one-eighth share to his son, Johannis, Jr., and his son-in-law, Charles Brodhead.

No conveyance has ever been found out of Governor Cornbury and the one-eighth shares for which record is available add up to a complete interest. Thus, it seems that Cornbury never held title to any part of or share in the Patent even though stories persisted that he did. Or else, Bickley hid that title so well it never appeared.

By 1751, Robert Livingston held a full one-eighth share, a one-half interest in three one-eighth shares, and a one-eighth interest in a one-eighth share, or just a little less than an overall one-third interest in the Hardenburgh Patent.

It is difficult to sort out the Livingstons because so many of them cross and recross the pages of the early history of the United States and, especially, of New York State. In the Catskills, it is even more difficult because the four who were most involved in the mountain land were all named Robert and two of them had the same middle initial, R. To make matters worse, the two daughters (and only children) of the fourth Robert each married a Livingston and one of them was also named Robert.

The Robert Livingston who acquired one-third of the Hardenburgh Patent was born in 1688, the son of the first Robert, who was also the first Livingston to come to the United States, arriving from Scotland at the age of twenty. The first Robert (1654-1728) was the son of a Presbyterian minister. He was a businessman, so the record states, but one of those businesses was, in partner with William III and several other respectable and powerful men of England, the financing of Captain William Kidd in a venture to plunder other pirates of their booty, transship it to Boston, and there sell it and divide the proceeds. But Kidd made the mistake of capturing vessels of the British East India Company of which some of his sponsors were members. The clamor raised compelled the group to abandon their plan for the time being and sacrifice Captain Kidd. On May 23, 1701, Kidd was hanged at Execution Dock in London and, according to the custom of the Admiralty, was left chained to a post on the shore until three tides washed over him.

Livingston's other "business' enjoyed better success. He courted and won the widow Alida Van Rensselaer (the daughter of Philip Schuyler). He then tried to gain control of the Colony of Rensselaerwyck, which amounted to over one million acres. The other members of the Van Rensselaer family soon saw what was going on and sent Livingston down the Hudson where he established Livingston Manor in Columbia County.

The Manor started out with a grant from the Crown to a tract of land on the Roelof Jansen Kill; however, Livingston soon petitioned for a second grant stating he had found the first one to be poor land, "very little being Fitt to be Improved." He got the second grant, a paltry six hundred acres, and, although it was some distance from the lands of the first grant, he was able to convince all and sundry that they did, in fact, adjoin. In time, his claim grew to encompass a tract of over 200,000 acres. In the later years of his life, he sat as Speaker of the New York Assembly (1718-1725) and served on the Governor's Council.

The Robert Livingston of the Hardenburgh Patent was a merchant and the builder (in 1730) of the manor house called Clermont on the east shore of the Hudson River, where it looked west to the Catskill Mountains and the Great Patent. It was for the manor house that Robert Fulton named his steamboat in recognition of the massive support—monetary and otherwise—given by the fourth Robert in the early 1800s. Robert of Clermont died in June of 1775, leaving his only son, Robert R., as his heir.

The third Robert Livingston was born in 1718 and served as Justice of the Supreme Court of New York from 1763 to 1775 and, thereafter, has always been referred to as Judge Livingston. He died in December of 1775, only six months after his father's death, leaving his wife, Margaret Beekman, and ten children. If the earlier generations of the Livingston family could be said to have been "well-connected," this generation could be put down as one that held the reins of the New York State and Federal governments.

Of the eleven children of the Judge; Janet married General Richard Montgomery, who was killed in the attack on Quebec in December of 1775; Robert R. was the first Chancellor of the State of New York; Margaret married Dr. Thomas Tillotson, who was the United States Secretary of State; Henry Beekman was a Brigadier-General during the Revolutionary War; Gertrude married Major-General Morgan Lewis, who later became Governor of New York (it was their daughter, Margaret, for whom the Village of Margaretville was named); Johanna married her cousin, Peter R. Livingston, who was State Senator and President of the Senate; Alida married General John Armstrong, who was United States Senator, Minister to France, and Secretary of War; and Edward was Mayor of New York City, United States Senator and Secretary of State, and the author of the Louisiana Code of Laws.

It was Chancellor Robert R. Livingston, the fourth Robert, who financed Fulton and his steamboat. He ran into Fulton in France while he (the Chancellor) was there as Minister to France, having been sent by Thomas Jefferson to negotiate the Louisiana Purchase. Actually, Jefferson sent the Chancellor to buy New Orleans, but he negotiated well and ended up with what became known as the Louisiana Purchase. He was one of five men appointed to draft the Declaration of Independence, was influential in bringing about New York State's adoption of the United States Constitution, served as Jefferson's Secretary of State, and, as Chancellor of New York State, administered the oath of office to George Washington at his inauguration as the first President of the United States.

The Chancellor was not a signer of the Declaration of Independence as is stated in some records — the Livingston who was one of the four signers from New York State was Phil. Livingston of another branch of the family. However, of the two statues that each State has placed in the rotunda of the Capitol at Washington, one of those from New York is of the Chancellor. The other is of George Clinton, the first Governor of New York State and a Vice-President of the United States, who once said of the Livingstons, "It is a vile family." Another source says, "The Livingston family, from the days of the infamous Livingston-Kidd and Company piratical partnership, were distinguished for self- proclaimed virtue in their methods of capitalizing upon the necessities of others."

An example of this is the Chancellor's gift of 5,000 acres to the people of the Town of Kingston following the burning of their homes by the British on October 16, 1777. The deed of gift states that the inhabitants of Kingston had "distinguished themselves by their patriotism and zeal in the Defence of the Rights and Liberties of their much injured and oppressed County, thereby rendering themselves peculiarly obnoxious to their British Foes." All this "excited the Benevolence and compassion" of the Chancellor, a "humane and generous friend to the American cause," and "influenced solely by the[se] motives" he wanted to "relieve the distressed Inhabitants" by giving them land on which to build new homes. Actually, the reason behind Livingston's generosity were a bit more circumspect.

The 5,000 acres was, of course, only a small part of the 500,000 acres then held by the Chancellor in the Hardenburgh Patent and was located way off in the wilderness some fifty miles from Kingston. In fact, the tract (now called New Kingston) was not settled until sixteen years after the burning of Kingston and the censuses of 1790 and 1800 do not list a single donation-allottee as living there. But the 5,000 acres was located between the East and West branches of the Delaware River and that area was the subject of a legal action at that time. If, reasoned the Chancellor, settlers moved onto the land, that would establish title into him by possession and occupation. Secondly, in order to reach the gift lands, roads would have to be improved or built all the way from Kingston (by the localities involved, of course) and the land along these roads — owned by the Chancellor — would become more valuable. In both cases, he was right.

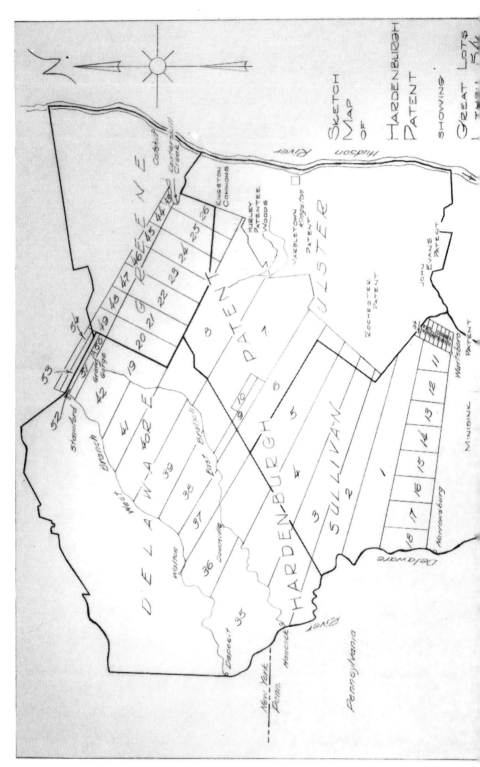

20

Chapter 3

The Early Surveyors

WHATEVER THE SHORTCOMINGS of the Livingstons, it was they and their one-third ownership in the Hardenburgh Patent that finally got it surveyed. Of course, once the Patent had been granted in 1708, the need for a survey to describe it was no longer important. It was not until 1753 that provisions were adopted requiring "a faithful and exact survey" before a patent could be granted. However, by 1721, enough problems had arisen at various places around the outbounds of the Patent that Attorney General Bickley petitioned the Governor for a survey—not a survey of the Hardenburgh Patent, but "of the Said Townes of Kingston or other the Said Patents as shall be thought Necessary to Ascertaine to the True bounds of yor petitioners Said Tract of land." The Governor ordered the Surveyor General to carry out the survey, but it appears not to have been done. In 1739, announcement was made that the Patent would be divided among the then owners, but with the number of boundary disputes raised by landowners in the adjoining patents and with the Indians still claiming (and rightfully so) they owned the land of the Patent, the division did not go forward. Clearly a survey was needed.

"Allowing for the Spherical form of the Earth and Protuberances of the Mountains," said one of the early surveyors, "[the Hardenburgh Patent] will contain upwards of one and one-half million acres." It was found to actually include 1,454,175 acres.

If it is difficult to keep the Robert Livingstons straight and in order, it is also difficult to sort out the original surveyors, even though only two of them were involved. Henry and Ebeneezer Wooster were brothers from Stamford, Connecticut. Sometimes the record calls for Henry as the land surveyor running such and such line; other times the record names Ebeneezer

21

as running that line; and, on occasion, the record speaks of "one Worster, the Surveyor" as being the one who ran the line.

It does appear that Henry was first in the field; however, the date when he was there had not been discovered with certainty. One source puts it as "in or about the year 1740." As a result of this survey, the two Indian deeds of 1746 were acquired, so the survey was prior to that. It was Johannis Hardenbergh himself who hired Henry Wooster and Hardenbergh conveyed his interest in the Patent to his son and son-in-law in 1743, so the survey was before that date. Whenever it was, Henry Wooster was sent off to run the southerly line of the Patent.

The 1746 deed from the Minisink Indians calls the southeast corner of the Patent as being "att a Certain Place in Ulster County. . .called hunting house or Yagh House, lying to the North East of the Land Called Bashes Land. . . ." Just where Henry began his survey is unclear, but he ran the line "West by North untill itt meet with the ffish kill or maine Branch of Delaware River." After some delays, brought about by confrontations with the Indians, Henry proceeded up the river to what is now Hancock and then ran up the East Branch of the Delaware River — called Pachatackhan in the 1746 deed from the Esopus Indians — "to the head thereof." There, Henry marked a spruce tree with three Xs. He was at the head of the long marshy area just southwest from Grand Gorge on the divide between the Delaware and Schoharie watersheds. He wanted to go west to establish the northwest corner of the Patent at the head of the West Branch of the Delaware River, but the Indians turned him east for home.

Next came Ebeneezer Wooster — he took to the field on April 7, 1749. Ebeneezer's charge was to complete the survey of the outbounds of the Patent in preparation for the partition between the eight interests that made up the title. He says, "I Began at the Cartrigeh Kill where made a Monument of Stone Round a crocked [crooked] Chestnut oak tree." His map calls the stream the Mohonenk Kill instead of Cartrigeh Kill, but it was one and the same. However, the major question of why Ebeneezer did not begin at "the head of a Certain Small River Commonly known by the Name of Cartwright's Kill" as called for in the grant of the Patent or at "the head of the Caterix Kill" as cited in the deed from the Esopus Indians still remains. He did, indeed, begin at the Cartwright's of Caterix Kill (known today as Kaaterskill Creek), but he was far from the head of it. He was actually at "the Northermost Bounds of Kingstown on the said Kill or River" as set out in the grant and called in the deed from the Esopus Indians as being at "the bounds of Kingston."

From this beginning (just west from what is now Palenville), Ebeneezer ran southerly along the westerly bounds of the various patents — Kingston Commons, Hurley Patentee Woods, Marbletown Patent, Rochester Patent, and John Evans Patent — that had earlier been granted on the west side of the Hudson River. He set sixteen stone monuments along the way with the last one being at the ". . .Great Yach House where we made a Monnt [Monument] of Stones and marked 3 white pine trees with No. XVI, about 3 Roods to the Northward of Minisinck Road."

Ebeneezer then ran northwesterly along the line put in by his brother, Henry, some thirty miles or so "To the Great Fish Kill" where he found "a black oak tree marked with...the old marks of Henry Wooster." He went up the river to the junction of the East and West branches and here, like his brother, met the Indians. The Indians claimed they had not sold the area between the two branches and forced Ebeneezer to continue his survey up the East Branch. He placed seventeen monuments as he went, some of which the Indians, following behind him, threw into the river.

Ebeneezer set his last monument at the northerly end of the two-mile-long marsh just south of Grand Gorge "at the old corner Bounds made by Henry Wooster a Spruce tree which he had marked with 3X. . .at the upper End of the Swamp...in between two high mountains against the Upper End of the mountains the Monument Stands."

With Ebeneezer Wooster on his survey crew was one Henry Bush "then of Shookan." Bush later told the story that after setting the seventeenth monument, they struck cross-country "in search of the another Branch of said River. . . .[T]hey came on another Stream which they pursued down" after either making or finding (Bush was not clear on this point) a canoe into which they loaded all their surveying equipment. At one point they "overset their Cannoe and wetted their Instruments, by which the Surveyor's Chain became exceedingly rusty." They continued down the river to the "Cookhurse [somewhere between Walton and Deposit] where they found many Indians who discovering that they had a Surveyor as also Instruments for surveying Lands were much enraged and talked of killing the whole party as they the said Indians claimed the Lands as their Property. — that Wooster and his Party diverted the Indians from their purpose by assuring them that they had not surveyed any of the Lands on that River, and in proof thereof shewed them the Rust on their Chain, which satisfied the Indians that they had not used it."

Although Ebeneezer did not close his survey by running the north line of the Patent and did not, other than the canoe trip down the West Branch, survey the west line, he did produce a map showing the entire Hardenburgh Patent.

The map broke the Patent into twenty-six great lots within the bounds of the lines run by Ebeneezer and a north line that ran from the two-mile swamp at Grand Gorge to his place of beginning on the Mohonenk or Cartrigeh Kill. In addition, Ebeneezer tacked on another sixteen great lots; eight at the southeast corner where a gap existed between the line he had run and the patent to the east and eight to the west of the East Branch of the Delaware River. None of these sixteen additional great lots had closing lines — the north and south lines of each hung suspended with no apparent end.

On November 8, 1749, a drawing by ballot was held and under the deed of partition dated November 15, the forty-two great lots were divided among the eight interests with six shares consisting of five great lots each and two shares consisting of six great lots each.

In an attempt to clear up any deficiencies in title caused by the fact that "one Worster, the Surveyor" hadn't run either the north or the west lines of the Patent and the still nagging problem of the Indians claiming they hadn't sold the land between the East and West branches of the Delaware River, the partitioners acquired a deed from the Papacton Indians (whether the proper indians signed the deed would continue to be a question) on June 3, 1751. This deed included the land between the two branches of the Delaware and the land lying southerly of a line running from the head of the West Branch easterly to "the head of Catricks-kill." This created another twelve great lots to the north of those shown on Ebeneezer's map. A second ballot drawing and a following partition deed (dated June 6, 1751) divided these great lots among the eight interests.

However, it was another fifty years before the final outbound lines of the Patent would be settled. The easterly line had to be adjusted along its entire length to conform with the lines of the earlier patents. It took a boundary line agreement and survey "run out A.D. 1776 by Will Cockburn" to finally establish the boundary between the Hardenburgh Patent and the Rochester Patent adjoining on the east.

The westerly line was not finally decided until 1786. Then, it took the intervention of Sir William Johnson and a long, drawn-out law suit to lay to rest the question of the Indian ownership, the claims of a number of squatters who contended they held title, and the rights of other adverse claiments who had gained some interest in the land between the two branches of the Delaware in the intervening years. Each side had their own surveyors, whose testimony was as much in conflict as were the claims. Some argued their research proved the East Branch to be the "ffish Kill or River" called for in the grant of the Patent. Others were just as positive that the West Branch was intended. One surveyor testified that he believed the Beaverkill was the "Kill or River" called for. The 1786 decision set the West Branch of the Delaware River as the westerly limit of the Hardenburgh Patent.

All that was left then was the north line. In the very beginning, the north line of the Hardenburgh Patent was to be what was then the line between the counties of Albany and Ulster. Neither Henry nor Ebeneezer Wooster had surveyed the north line in their surveys in the 1740s. The first surveyors to go on the ground to establish it were William Cockburn and Cadwallader

Colden in 1765. Later surveys found they had located the line too far to the north.

However, the first two attempts set the limits for the line—the Cockburn/Colden line being the northerly limit and the line on Ebeneezer Wooster's map running from his point of beginning just westerly of Palenville to his seventeenth monument at the marsh at Grand Gorge being the southerly limit. The true north line lay somewhere between the two and a number of surveyors and government officials had a try at establishing it.

John Cox, in 1787, began at a point on the small stream that ran from North Lake to South Lake, taking that as the head "of Cartwright's Kill," and ran northwesterly to the headwaters of the Delaware. There, he accepted the point (upstream from Lake Utsayantha) that Ebeneezer Wooster had struck when he went cross-country from the seventeenth monument at Grand Gorge. This point is noted on a map of the period as "Here Woorster makes the Head of the Delaware."

Christopher Tappan and James Cockburn (the son of William) next entered the field under the authority of a law passed by the State Legislature on March 29, 1790, for the purpose of "surveying and establishing certain lines and dividing certain Lots in the Hardenburgh Patent." As a part of their task, they needed to establish the north line of Great Lot 49. Here they found the Cox line of three years earlier and ran their line "along the north line of the Patent as run by John Cox in the year 1787."

The next surveyors were Alexander Daniels and James Cockburn, Jr. They were in the field in 1844 "by Order of the Surveyor General" for the purpose of establishing "The Division Between Schoharie & Delaware County." They established their final line along a straight line running from Lake Utsayantha to the outlet of South Lake.

The north line is a combination of the Cox, Tappan & Cockburn, and Daniels & Cockburn surveys and is not a single, "Direct Line" as called for in the grant of the Patent. No matter, the Hardenburgh Patent was finally encircled by a surveyed line. And, by then also, much of the interior of the Patent had been surveyed, and divided into smaller and smaller lots.

The surveyors who laid out the interior great lot, tract, and lot lines of the Patent were also a hardy bunch and, according to the record, accomplished much in a short time. Jonas Smith surveyed some 15,000 acres of Great Lot 22 into over 100 lots noting on his map "Surveyed and Laid into Lots in the Month of June AD 1795." John Wigram, surveying in Great Lot 21 to the west found the land in the south part of it so rugged it was not worth dividing into lots. His map says of this area "3100 a[cres] Vacant— South part sold—Centre very rough & wild - Road goes through it."

Not only did the surveyors have trouble running out and finding the various boundary lines, so too did the early settlers. The Wigram map notes "The four Lots No. 19, 20, 21 & 22 stained Yellow were sold in 1787 to

Frederic Augustus DeZeng and were purchased from Edward Livingston, viz: Lots No. 19, 20 & 21 by Elijah Bushnell, Elijah Bushnell, jun. & Aaron Bushnell, who having settled upon the wrong Lot, the lot stained blue was released to him in lieu of Lot No. 20."

It was the land adjoining these Bushnell lots and consisting of the 3,100 acres "rough & wild" that was "sold" to Chauncey Musgrave by Edward Livingston. Just what Musgrave's relationship was, if any, to the Livingston family is unclear. He was obviously English (the name could be of no other heritage). The speculation is that he may have been associated with Chancellor Robert R. Livingston during the time the Chancellor was in France. The record title to the 3,100 acres shows that it wasn't "sold" to Musgrave, it was, instead, "a gift out of the kindness of my [Edward Livingston's] heart to my friend, faithful and true." Musgrave never saw his land because he never came to the United States. The deed that conveyed the 3,100 acres gives his place of residence as London. The only parcel broken out and sold by Musgrave was to Caleb Ford and that remained with the Ford family for generations.

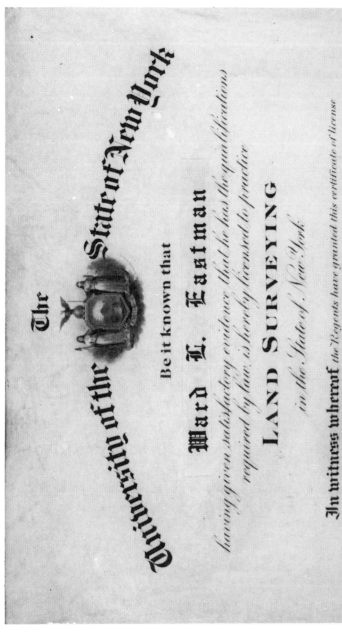

The

University of the State of New York

Be it known that

Ward L. Eastman

having given satisfactory evidence that he has the qualifications
required by law, is hereby licensed to practice

LAND SURVEYING

in the State of New York.

In witness whereof the Regents have granted this certificate of license
number 1396 under the seal of the University this 12th day of September 1922

President of the University

State Board of Licensing for
Professional Engineers and Land Surveyors

Albert H. Hooker
Chairman
George R. Balen
Vice-Chairman
Virgil M. Palmer
Allen L. Clark
Henry F. Rent

28

Chapter 4

Ward Eastman, Land Surveyor

IT WAS AGAINST THIS BACKGROUND of patents and great lots, boundary lines and hardy individuals, that Ward Eastman set his goal in life to be a land surveyor, that he might follow the "tracks" left by those who had surrounded the Catskill Mountains with surveys and had blocked out the ridges and valleys within into tracts and lots, great and otherwise.

Ward was born at the turn of the century in the rural town of Jewett at the northeastern corner of the Catskills. His father scraped a living from a rockbound farm in the shadow of the Blackhead Range. While farming may have been his living, his renown was in his skill as a bear hunter. "Aaron Eastman never loses a bear once he gets on its trail," said the old-timers around the pot-bellied stove down at Ed Hill's general store. The workings of the Eastman farm came to a standstill when the air turned cold in the late fall and snow flurried over the high peaks of the mountains. Then, Aaron filled his old, tattered, canvas rucksack with the barest of necessities, a stock of ammunition, an extra wool shirt or two, strapped a pair of snowshoes on the outside and headed into the hills, not to be seen until days later when he appeared from another direction dragging the black-furred carcass of a bear behind him.

Aaron Eastman hunted bear the year 'round; however, it was only in the early winter just before den-up time that he carried his rifle into the woods. The rest of the year he roamed the ridges of the high Catskills, seeking out signs of the bear, searching for the obvious dens where they would hole up for the winter, and finding their wallows and routes of travel. When late fall came, he was as much a bear as the bear was and knew more of their comings and goings than he did about where the stock was on his farm. "If bear

29

hunting was a paying proposition, Aaron Eastman would be a millionaire twice over," said the old-timers down at the store. However, it wasn't, and he remained a poor farmer who didn't care whether the cows came home or not.

In contrast, Ward's mother was the most dependable woman in town. Nellie Baldwin had been born and raised in the neighboring town of Hunter. When she and Aaron got to the courting stage, her parents despaired for her future. She would never get to be a school teacher as she had dreamed, they said, and Aaron Eastman would never provide a fit support for her. They were wrong on the first count, but right on the second.

Nellie Eastman was the teacher in the little one-room school house that sat beside the road next door to the Eastman home. "And," said the ladies down at the church hall, "She hasn't missed a day of school since she started teaching there just a week after she and Aaron got married." She went to school they said, and Aaron headed for the mountains looking for bear. Ward was born during the summer, so Nellie didn't have to take time off from school for his birth although a lot of tongues wagged up and down the valley as she continued to teach right through the time it became obvious she was "with child." "Did you ever?" said the ladies. "Why, it's scandalous, her still teaching, standing up there in front of those children. Why, you'd think the school board would do something about it." Well, they didn't. Nellie kept on teaching and the world didn't fall apart after all.

The same ladies started wringing their hands in the fall when school began again because Nellie bundled Ward in his blanket, put him in an old peach basket, and carried him off to school every day. He spent the hours of school on the floor beside her desk and the children loved it. He was quiet and content and seemed to listen to all that was being said, absorbing the knowledge along with the class being taught at the moment. When he became old enough to start first grade, he seemed ahead of the other students and little wonder, he had heard the same subjects taught before, some of them as many as five times.

All the local residents were sure that Aaron Eastman would be about as good a father as he was a farmer, but they were wrong on that one. The very first fall of Ward's life, Aaron loaded him into the old rucksack, wrapped him in the extra shirts, and carried him off into the hills. Nellie had every confidence all would be well and it was. When they returned four days later, Ward's cheeks were a robust pink, his eyes were bright, and his stomach was full; with what Nellie didn't ask.

Thereafter, Ward accompanied his father on at least one bear hunt every fall and at other times throughout the year on Aaron's scouting treks. It was during these times he learned how to read the woods, pace himself as he climbed up and down the mountains, and, especially, appreciate the hard-won vistas from the high peaks. He found his father to be a sensitive man, extremely knowledgeable about the natural world, and not at all the ne'er-do-well others thought him to be. Away from the confines of walls, fences, and other shackles, he was an expert in what he did. He taught Ward a respect for the woods and the land that could not have been learned any other way.

Nellie Eastman was the self-appointed town historian. She visited 'round and about, rummaged in people's memories and attics, and accumulated a vast store of information about the settlements in the town, how they had come to be, who the settlers were, where they had come from, and what had drawn them to this secluded and remote part of the world to begin with. She went to the country seat at Catskill and looked through the old deed and mortage records on file there and discovered a treasure trove of maps and fieldnotes of the early surveyors who had passed through the mountains. Ward, of course, went along on these excursions and was fascinated by the stories told by the older residents. He became adept at searching out deeds for parcels of land and running the chains of title from the present ownerships back to the Livingstons.

The three of them, Ward, his mother, and his father, sometimes became an amateur survey crew. Occasionally, an old-timer would tell about a family who had once lived up one of the deeper valleys, or high on one of the ridges, or at some other location in town that was completely grown over by dense forests. Nellie and Ward would then go to Catskill, look up the deeds covering land the family had owned, copy out the descriptions of the parcels included in those deeds and in the deeds of the properties adjoining, and trace off any old survey maps they could find that covered the area involved. Armed with that information, they had Aaron locate the land for them.

Aaron, in addition to his complete understanding of the lay of the land, had an unerring sense of direction that depended on the shadows made by the sun, the feel of the wind on his face, and a dead-reckoning by which he could walk a straight line for miles regardless of the terrain. He did, however, always carry a hand compass and early on taught Ward how to use it. With that and by pacing off distances as they went, they followed stone walls, remains of wire fences, and blazes faintly visable on the old line trees until they located the piles of stones set by the original surveyors to mark the corners of the property.

With the property thus laid out on the ground, they crisscrossed it until they could place the outlines of the fields and pastures that once constituted the farmland and the tracks of the old roadways the farmer used long before in working the land. They usually located the cellar hole or the remains of an old house foundation in some spot that would be warmed by the early morning sun; what better way to break the chill of a winter's night in the Catskills. If they could find no other sign of the spot where the farmhouse once stood, Aaron would admonish them to look for a lilac bush—"The farmer's wife always planted a lilac bush by the back door," he said, "so she could enjoy the smell and sight of its blossoms as she went about her work in the kitchen; it was about the brightest thing she could hope for in her otherwise drab life."

Invariably, he was right; whenever they found a lilac bush, they scraped away the leaves and duff nearby, and usually uncovered the remains of the old foundation. If the time of day was right, this was where they ate their lunch that had been carried all morning on Ward's back in the old, tattered, canvas rucksack that Aaron had passed down to him. "The farmer's wife would be pleased to have us enjoy a meal in her kitchen," Aaron said, and he was right about that, too.

Nellie taught Ward the intricacies of trigonometry and how to transfer the compass bearings and paced distances to grid lines on paper to produce a map of the properties they located. With this training, Ward Eastman came to understand the land surveyor's methods at an early age. He became interested in the Hardenburgh Patent and the shenanigans that set it out in a single grant and those manipulations that followed bringing title to much of it into the Livingstons. Nellie took him to Albany, by the West Shore Railroad from Catskill, where they searched for the original patent and the fieldnotes and maps of the Woosters and the other early surveyors. It was a tedious business copying out all that material with its antiquated spelling and syntax, but they did it although it took them more than a few trips to complete the task. In the end, they had as much of the story of the Patent in their files as was in any other single file in Albany or elsewhere.

The Eastman house and farm was just inside the Hardenburgh Patent; in fact, the north line of the farm was also the north line of the Patent, marked at that point by a stone wall. In the spring of Ward's fourteenth year, he and his father traversed, with their hand compasses, the entire thirty-five miles of the north line of the Patent, beginning at the outlet of North Lake and running northwesterly to Lake Utsayantha above Stamford.

The years of Ward Eastman's growing up were memorable, pleasant, and a time of learning, both from books and by experience. His was an education not to be matched anywhere else at the time. However, it all came to an abrupt end one early morning in the middle of the winter of 1917-18. Whether a down-draft caused the kitchen stove to explode or what, no one could ever be sure, but explode it did. Aaron and Nellie slept in the room off the kitchen and they weren't able to escape the flames that quickly enveloped that end of the house. Ward, who slept in the upstairs room at the other end of the house, was able to jump from a window. He could only watch the house burn to the ground as he stood in the snow, the cold, and the darkness of that winter morning. And his world crumbled too; all was lost, even the records of the Hardenburgh Patent that he and Nellie had so laboriously copied and the old tattered rucksack that Aaron had carried for so many years and so many miles.

For a time after that, Ward seemed to drift aimlessly like a ship at sea with its sheet anchor gone. He had no other home to go to; his mother and father had been only children as was he, so he had no aunts and uncles to take him in. The local folks were saddened also and many offered him bed and board in their homes. However, having been brought up to be of an independent mind, he declined those kind gestures. He rented a couple of furnished rooms up over Ed Hill's store down on the corner and went to work for Jack Kline cutting logs on the estate at the head of the valley.

As spring approached, he heard the State was hiring men to work on the two crews that surveyed the lines of the State-owned land in the Adirondacks. The one crew that worked surveying the State land in the Catskills was full. However, he had known Lawrence McKee, the man in charge of that crew, for the past few years and asked if he would recommend him to his colleagues in the Adirondacks. Armed with that letter of recommendation and carrying all his meager belongings, he took the West Shore to Albany. Evidently, McKee had sent word ahead that Ward would be an asset to the State land surveying force, because the interview with the head land surveyor in the headquarters at the State Capitol went quickly. Ward was promptly hired and sent on by the next northbound train with orders to report to the surveyor in charge of the crew at Saranac Lake.

The next few years went quickly. He liked the Adirondacks and found the survey work there to be the same as that in the Catskills. The boundary lines were marked on the ground with blazed trees and the corners were similar piles of stones. He learned much from the irascible old surveyor he worked with and quickly realized that as long as he did what was expected of him, he was treated with respect — he never earned a compliment from the surveyor, but no one else ever did either. Many had, however, been berated by him and, since Ward wasn't, he figured he was doing all right.

Ward sat for his license in 1922 and got it. He also courted the young school teacher at the one-room schoolhouse just down the road from the survey office once he got up his courage to do so. He needn't have worried; their attraction was mutual. Ward didn't broach the idea of marriage until after he received his license to practice land surveying, but they were married soon after. The wedding was a small affair since neither of them had any close family.

A couple of years later, word came that Lawrence McKee had died suddenly from a heart attack. The head office in Albany told Ward to report to Fleischmanns in Delaware County and take over responsibility for the survey crew headquartered there. At first, he was reluctant to go. When he left the Catskills he had vowed never to return because he didn't want to travel those hills and valleys where he surely would cross the paths he, his mother, and his father had walked together; he didn't want to stir the memories of the sad time of their passing. However, Betty, his wife, convinced him that not all his Catskill memories were bad ones and that the good ones should not be forgotten.

So, Ward Eastman returned to the southern hills of his youth. He and Betty found a small house that matched their meager, State- employee budget just up Woodland Valley not far from the hamlet of Phoenicia and only about fifteen miles from the State office in Fleischmanns. However, he didn't really see that much of the office. The survey crew was then involved in a frantic effort surveying the many parcels of land being acquired under the provisions of a bond act that had been approved by the voters in 1916 to add to the State-owned Forest Preserve in the Adirondack and Catskill mountains. When the money was finally all spent in 1927, nearly 49,000 acres had been added to the Catskill Forest Preserve and all of it had to be surveyed. This task carried Ward and his crew all over the high peaks of the Catskills as all or parts of Hunter, West Kill, High Point, Mount Tremper, Blackhead, Thomas Cole, Plateau, Twin, Sugarloaf, Indian Head, and Belleayre mountains were purchased by the State under this program.

It was while surveying the newly-acquired State lands on Blackhead and Thomas Cole mountains that Ward visited, for the first time since the winter of 1917-18, the land where he had grown up and the graves of his mother and father. He had since sold the land and saw that a new house had been built on the foundation of the home of his early years. He was glad the charred remains were gone.

It was with funds from the 1916 bond act that the State purchased the old Musgrave property. The 3,100 acres had been reduced by the 320 acres or so that had been sold to Caleb Ford back in the early 1800s. At the time of the State purchase, the 2,780 acres remaining was owned by a man named Craig, who had built a house in the middle of the property at the roughest and wildest part and next to the road that "goes through it." It was then that Ward Eastman first walked the lines of the Ford farm.

Long before the lands acquired with the 1916 monies had been surveyed, another bond act was approved by the voters of New York State. The funds from the 1924 bond act lasted until 1944 and over 72,000 acres were purchased for addition to the Catskill Forest Preserve. One of these acquisitions amounted to nearly 2,000 acres and included the entire of North Lake. While surveying this property, Ward again visited the pile of stones at the outlet of the lake that marked the northeast corner of the Hardenburgh Patent and the point where he and his father had started their trek across the long north line of the Patent years before.

The pace of State land surveys slowed in the 1940s as the war intervened and funds from the earlier bond acts were depleted. Land acquisition monies were harder to come by then, with specific purchases and the funds

34

for them being programmed through the regular State-budget process. Still, survey of the State land boundaries continued as the adjoining private lands were developed or lumbered. The lines needed to be well-established in order to prevent trespass from these lands over onto the public lands. In time, Ward Eastman ran part of at least one of the lines of each of the great lots of the Hardenburgh Patent. He felt great pleasure and satisfaction in finding corners that had been set by "one Worster, the Surveyor" and other of the early surveyors and in following the dim "tracks" of them along lines of ancient blazed trees and tumbling stone walls. He became known as *the* Catskills surveyor and was well-liked and respected by all, except for one of his neighbors, who told those who would listen, "Don't trust that Eastman's surveys because he's moved every corner between here and the Delaware River." Which branch, the East or the West, he didn't say.

In 1959, planning was begun to formulate another bond act to be presented to the voters at the 1960 general election. Ward decided he wasn't going to endure the fast pace of another accelerated land purchasing program and opted, instead, for retirement. After all, over forty years of working for a public bureaucracy was enough for anyone. So, he left State service in the spring of 1961 just as the new land acquisition program started.

He did not, however, retire from land surveying; he derived too much enjoyment from his profession to give that up. Ever since he had returned to the Catskills in 1925, he had run a private business on Saturdays and holidays. He usually employed a couple of the young men from the State survey crew for this "outside" work for which they were thankful, because they found the near-poverty wages paid by the State weren't enough to keep and raise a family. Betty taught school and proved to be an excellent map-maker; it was she who drafted most of the maps of those private surveys over the years. Now she, too, retired and, along with Ward, became the nucleus of the full-time, private, land-surveying business.

Over the years, in addition to Betty and the men from the State survey crew, Ward employed a couple of other young people for the summer months, who worked during the week doing research into the deed records in the county clerk's offices and in the field brushing out transit lines for the survey work to be done the following Saturday. Four of these, as time went on, were the children of Larry Ford, the shiftless half of the Ford twins, and that "gypsy woman" he ran off with.

THIS INDENTURE, Made the Sixteenth day of January in the year of our Lord one thousand eight hundred and two **BETWEEN** Chauncey Musgrave of London, England, of the first part, and Caleb Ford of South Branch in the Town of Windham, County of Greene and State of New York of the second part.

Witnesseth, that the said party of the first part, in consideration of the sum of Two hundred dollars to me duly paid and in further consideration of good and faithful service to me given, hath sold, and **By These Presents,** doth grant and convey to the said party of the second part, his heirs and assigns, ALL that certain piece or parcel of land lying and being in the town of Windham aforesaid in Great Lot 21 Hardenburgh Patent bounded as follows, **Beginning** in the center of the South Branch where the same is crossed by the line of lands of Tomlinson & Day and runs southwesterly along said lands about 88 chains to a stone pile set against the mountain, thence northwesterly through lands of the party of the first part about 36 chains and two rods to a stone pile on the mountain, thence northeasterly continuing through lands of the said party of the first part herein for part of the way and then running along lands now or once owned by Frederic DeZeng a distance of about eighty-eight chains to the center of said Branch, thence up said Branch to the place where this land started, containing about three hundred and twenty acres. **Together with** one half of the water of the spring on lands of said party of the first part in back of the above lands and further up the mountain and the right to run the same to said lands. **With the Appurtenances,** and all the Estate, Title and Interest therein of the said party of the first part. And the said Chauncey Musgrave does hereby covenant and agree to and with the said party of the second part his heirs and assigns, that the premises thus conveyed in the Quiet and Peaceable Possession of the said party of the second part his heirs and assigns he will forever Warrant and Defend against any person whomsoever, lawfully claiming the same, or any part thereof.

In Witness Whereof, The party of the first part, has hereunto set his hand and seal the day and year first above written.

Chapter 5

The Fords

CALEB FORD CAME TO THE VALLEY of the South Branch "in the Month of June AD 1795" as an axman on the survey crew of Jonas Smith. He was about thirty years of age at the time (the records are unclear as to the year of his birth and just where he came from, although most suggest he was born in 1765 someplace in Connecticut). The story goes that the first time he set eyes on the land in Great Lot 21 of the Hardenburgh Patent that adjoined the lands being surveyed by Smith in Great Lot 22, Ford decided that was where he wanted to live. That took some doing because the land was already owned by Chauncey Musgrave and by Frederic DeZeng, they having acquired it from Edward Livingston. However, that didn't deter him. He came up with Musgrave's address somehow and wrote asking his permission to live on part of the land in exchange for watching over the entire 3,100 acres and protecting it from others who might take advantage of his absentee ownership. To this arrangement Musgrave agreed and Ford returned from wherever it was he then lived, accompanied by a wife nobody locally knew he had, a team of horses, six cows, and a wagon full of household furnishings.

It was Caleb who began to clear the land on the valley floor along the South Branch. The first clearing was on a flat knoll set back about 500 feet south of the stream. With lumber he sawed from the trees felled in the clearing, Caleb built the first house of the Ford family. As he cleared other lands, he built a barn and the usual array of outbuildings that went with a farm. The massive rocks he pried from the ground and hauled on stone boats to the building sites made a firm foundation for generations of farm buildings in the years that followed.

Caleb built the stone walls that ran, straight as an arrow, up the mountain on both sides of the farm. The wall on the east boundary marked the division line between Great Lots 21 and 22 of the Hardenburgh Patent and was an extension southerly of the westerly line of the lots laid out by Jonas Smith and his survey crew. Caleb understood the mysteries of the swinging needle of the compass from his work with Smith and other surveyors and the lines he laid out to mark the boundary of the farm stood the test of time.

A son, Jacob, was born to Caleb and his wife in 1800 and it was then Caleb decided he needed something more permanent than a tenancy on land that belonged to someone else. Along with the report he sent to Musgrave in London at the end of that year, he wrote a letter expressing his wish to purchase about three hundred acres or so on the northerly slopes of the mountain and south of the Branch. Again, Musgrave was agreeable. His only condition was that Caleb continue to watch over his remaining lands and report every year as usual on the state of them. So it was that a deed was drawn, based on measurements made by Caleb, and, in January of 1802, just two years after the county of Greene (spelled Green in the text of the law) was set out, Caleb Ford became the real owner of the lands he had cleared and the buildings he had raised.

The farm prospered over the years of the 1800s as well as any farm in the Catskills could. The best crop seemed to be stones. No matter how many were carried from the fields in the spring and used to build walls along the boundaries of the farm and between the numerous fields that checker-boarded the flats and the lower slopes of the mountain, an equal number appeared to sprout over the following winter to cover the fields again the next spring. But the Fords were industrious folks and, with a sense of humor, somewhere down the line named their land "Big Rock Farm." No one was ever sure whether the name came from the big rock that balanced on the brink of the high ledge way up the mountain or if it was because the land was more a rock farm than anything else and a big one at that.

Jacob succeeded to the farm when he came of age and added to the house when he married one of the Bushnell girls. Caleb and his wife continued to live in the house until they passed on in the cold winter of 1835. The cycle repeated when Orlando Ford, who was born in 1829, the only son and child of Jacob and his wife, took over the running of the farm in the late 1850s. Orlando married Ada Maben and their only child, Josiah, was born in 1860.

Ward Eastman felt as if he knew Josiah Ford, mostly because he had been a bear hunter and sometimes hunted with his father, Aaron. He didn't really recall Josiah, but he did remember, in the very early years of his life, that Josiah Ford had stopped in many times at the Eastman house on his way to a bear hunt or on his way back. It would have been early in Ward's life because Josiah Ford was swept downstream when the big flood in the spring of 1906 undermined the bank of the South Branch where he was standing.

His body was found five miles away, below Lexington, when the waters receded.

However, Ward recalled the stories Aaron told about Josiah Ford after the flood and before Aaron perished in the fire in 1918. Josiah was not much interested in farming; he wanted only to roam the hills, hunt bear in the winter and deer in the fall, go fishing in the spring, and read books in the summer. Perhaps that's why Josiah Ford and Aaron Eastman were friends.

When Josiah Ford was twenty years old, he left home and took a job as gamekeeper on the 8,000-acre estate of Samuel Huntington over in the remote country at the head of the Beaverkill in southwestern Ulster County. It was the ideal job for a person of Josiah's likes and dislikes. He came to know the 8,000 acres better than any of the Huntingtons, who came to the country only in the summer. The rest of the year they spent abroad or in the city where Samuel managed his far-flung holdings of railroads and mining lands in the west. During the other nine months of the year, Josiah roamed the 8,000-acre tract as if it were his own. In the snows of early winter, he often went overland to Jewett where he and Aaron Eastman tracked the black bear for days on end. Aaron used to say that Josiah Ford was the only man who could outwalk him up and down the mountains.

The Huntingtons took a great liking to Josiah Ford. They provided him with a house to live in on the estate and encouraged his interest in books and literature. He had free access to the vast library in the Huntington's main lodge and read everything there from Shakespeare to Dickens, from Chaucer to Poe, from William Blake to Ambrose Bierce. In time, he accumulated a library of his own, built up through gifts of books from the Huntingtons. He also took a wife, Sarah Todd, the pert young daughter of the Huntington's cook. In 1890, twin boys were born to Josiah and Sarah, breaking the tradition of generations of a single man-child being the only offspring in the Ford family.

In 1900, Orlando Ford died and Josiah's mother called him home to run the family farm. This didn't set well with Josiah. He wasn't a farmer he said and he really didn't have any interest in what happened to the farm. However, in the end, his mother prevailed, aided and abetted by Josiah's wife and by Samuel Huntington, who, although sorry to lose him as a valued employee, encouraged Josiah to set down roots on his own land and hold it together so the twins could succeed to it.

The farm had declined in the last decade of the 1800s. Orlando, in his sixties and running it alone, had sold off much of the stock, which meant less use of the pastures and the cutting of less hay to carry through the winter. As a result, the fields grew up to brush, the stones weren't picked up, the gardens got smaller, and the barn roof didn't get shingled when it should have. When Josiah took over the farm, things didn't improve much. He continued to fish in the spring, hunt in the fall, track bear in the winter, and added to his library the year 'round, expanding it to include the more current writers such as Twain, Conan Doyle, O. Henry, and Crane.

Had it not been for Sarah and the twins, the farm would have turned into a woodlot. Sarah saw to the gardens, kept the house spotless inside and out, and purchased a flock of chickens to start a small, but profitable, egg business. The twins, although only ten at the time the family came to the farm, kept the rest of it from going downhill any further. When Josiah lost his life in the flood, the farm was being run, for all intents and purposes, by Jerry Ford, the more sensible of the twins. His brother, Larry, had begun to exhibit his father's traits. As they grew older, the differences between them became more pronounced.

Some said the twins were eccentric. Others said they were born eccentric. Some said that if the twins were eccentric, then so were half the people in the valley because they all acted the same.

As far as being the same, the twins weren't. They were as different as night and day—not at all the way twins were supposed to be. Jerry ("His name is Gerald," his mother used to say. "Don't call him Jerry." But everyone did.) was quiet, didn't want to be around people (or didn't want people around him), believed in a good day's work, was neat as a pin, and kept everything around the farm in good-working order. If it was time to change the oil in the tractor, Jerry changed it; if it was time to feed the chickens, Jerry fed them; if it was time to take down the screen door and put up the storm door for winter, Jerry did that. Jerry never married; he didn't want anyone around to clutter up his life.

On the other hand, Larry ("His name is Lawrence," his mother used to say. "Don't call him Larry." But everyone did.) was the life of the party and if he couldn't find a party, he started one. Larry thought work was something to consider only when there was nothing else to do and didn't believe in picking up his clothes, his tools, or even his mail. ("All Larry ever picks up is girls," Jerry used to say.) Larry was always on the look-out for anything that took care of itself. He thought Pecos Bill's perpetual-motion ranch was just the thing. "Maybe we can get the farm to run like that," Larry suggested to Jerry, but Jerry only snorted and shook his head. If it was time to change the oil in the tractor, Larry said, "Let's get a new tractor." If it was time to feed the chickens, Larry said, "Let's sell 'em." If it was time to take down the screen door and put up the storm door for winter, Larry said, "Let's wait 'til spring and then we won't have to change back again."

People weren't really sure whether or not Larry ever married, but they knew he had run off with five or six women—not all at once, of course. Those capers out of the valley varied considerably in length of time. Once, the woman (that was Bill Gates' wife) was back the next day. However, when Larry left with the gypsy woman and her caravan (that he had let camp in the back pasture), he was gone for fifteen years. ("She put a curse on him," his mother said.) "I saw the world," Larry said when he came home, "but I didn't like it."

Larry drank a lot and Jerry was a tea-totaler. Jerry went to church and Larry didn't. ("I ain't never been churched," Larry used to say.) Jerry got up early every morning and Larry slept until noon or after. They didn't even look alike as twins were supposed to and nobody could figure that out.

The twins had been a surprise to their father. Sarah had wanted children, but Josiah didn't. Twins were a rarity in the valley—no one could remember another set—and their mother treated them as something special. When they were small, she made two of everything and tried to make Lawrence and Gerald into an identical pair every time she dressed them, but it didn't last long. Within an hour—even when they were babies—Lawrence's outfit was rumpled and twisted and messy while Gerald looked like he had just stepped out of a magazine advertisement.

As the boys grew older, it was obvious they had to have separate rooms. Gerald said he couldn't stand to look at the mess on Lawrence's side of their bedroom. Lawrence said it was all right with him if Gerald wanted to keep his side of the room neat; however, that didn't mean he had to pick up every sock or book or whatever as soon as he was done with it. So they each got their own room. When they did, the rule was that Gerald could leave his door open, but Lawrence had to keep his closed.

When Lawrence ran off with the gypsy woman ("She seduced him," his mother used to say.), his going broke his mother's heart. She even took to leaving his bedroom door open and the light on just in case he came home in the middle of the night (as he usually had in times past). She sat on the porch every day in the summer hoping to see him coming home; in the winter, she sat by the front window in the living room and watched down the long driveway waiting for him to appear. About a month after Lawrence had gone, the mailman delivered a postcard from him—by then he was three states away. After that, a card came every month—not regularly, of course, but nearly so. None ever gave a return address so they had no way of writing back to him.

A post card every month was not enough for Lawrence's mother and she slowly faded. She died five years later. Josiah's will had left the farm to the twins so that they each held a joint interest in the total property, subject, however, to a life use for Sarah with the stipulation that the twins were to care for their mother until her death. Of course, this had been left up to Jerry what with Larry off with the gypsies. The estate also held an amount of cash that Sarah had saved from the egg business over the years and that was divided equally between the twins—Larry's share was put in a bank account waiting for his return.

Since Larry wasn't there, Jerry used the whole property, but always deposited half of any profit in Larry's bank account. Jerry didn't have any way of telling Larry about the death of their mother although the post cards kept coming every month — or nearly so. Jerry threw them away, "with the rest of the junk mail," he said.

Fifteen years after he left (it was just a week before their thirty-sixth birthday), Larry came home. Jerry wasn't very happy to see him — the post cards had been enough for him.

If Jerry and the folks up and down the valley were surprised when Larry came back, they were absolutely shocked by what he brought with him. He wasn't alone. He had four children; James was thirteen, William was eleven, Maria was ten, and Carmen was eight. Where the gypsy woman and her caravan were, Larry never said and nothing was ever heard from her. The children were, for all intents and purposes, motherless and, for most of the time, fatherless too. Jerry, however, filled the gap — where first he resented them and the upset they brought to his well-ordered and single life, he came quickly to accept them almost as if they were his own. The children, sensing his feelings toward them, accepted him the same way.

Although Larry was home, it didn't make much difference in the running of the farm. If anything, it was more difficult. Larry's day still didn't begin until noon and that irritated Jerry no end. Jerry was the one who fed and watered the cows and milked them and kept them and the stables clean. It was Jerry who fixed the fences, tended the garden, and made sure all the equipment around the farm was maintained and worked the way it was supposed to. Jerry was always tinkering, always making some modification or adjustment or addition to the mowing machine, the hay rake, the stables, or the tractor to make each more efficient. Running the farm was a full-time, one-man job and Jerry thought it was a darn good thing because only one man was around to do it and when he thought about it, he fumed over that. It didn't do any good, because Larry went on his merry way although when Jerry kept at him all the time that irritated him no end.

The business of the twins sharing the house was also a losing game. Jerry had converted it into kind of a bachelor's quarters and had closed off a lot of the upstairs rooms because he just didn't need them. When Sarah died, Jerry reinstated the closed-door rule for Larry's room. He did all his own cooking and cleaning. He went down to the village to do some shopping now and then and even drove as far as the county seat in Catskill once in a while when he had farm business to attend to there. He visited with the villagers when he was on these journeys out into the world, but kept such visits to a minimum. The only exception was the local lads he hired on at busy times of the year to help with the work of the farm. He really enjoyed his way of life. Then Larry came home.

Jerry knew the house was jointly owned by him and Larry and that they were going to have to share it. However, the sharing got off on the wrong foot. Larry came through the front door that evening of his return and announced, "I'm home." He threw his suitcase on the floor at the foot of the stairs (where it was still the next morning), asked "What've you got to eat?" went on into the kitchen without waiting for an answer and got what he wanted out of the refrigerator, left the dirty dishes on the kitchen table, and went upstairs to bed. When Jerry went up later, he noticed the door to Larry's room was open. He knew then for sure that the good times were over.

The four children were left pretty much to fend for themselves and, from the way they went at it, were obviously used to it. The work of living was divided between them; Jim was in charge, made sure all did their schoolwork, and delegated tasks to the other three. Maria fixed the meals, Carmen washed the dishes, Bill did the cleaning; it was almost as if they were separate from their father — he went his way and they went theirs. Jerry enrolled them in school and sent them off to Sunday school down at the church in the village. Still, Jerry didn't want to take on the full responsibility of raising four children; he and his mother had failed with Larry and he had no confidence he would fare any better this time around.

Jerry did the best he could, but things just didn't work out. He found Larry's clothes mixed in with his when he did his laundry, most of the food he bought was gone when he went to fix his meals, and Larry never closed his bedroom door. The topper was one morning when he came in from the barn and found a woman standing stark-naked at the stove cooking bacon and eggs. Jerry was shocked, but the woman only said, "Hi, you want some breakfast?" and went on cooking. Right then he knew changes had to be made.

Jerry told Larry he was going to hire a carpenter and a plumber and an electrician and cut the house in two. (Well, not literally.) Larry said he didn't much care one way or the other. When the remodeling was done, the house consisted of two separate homes, each with its own entrance, although a door had been left in one inside wall so the children could go from one living room to the other without going outside. They came to spend as much time with Jerry as in their own side of the house and Jerry found he didn't really mind after all. As they grew older, they took on more and more of the work of running the farm.

However, even that couldn't last. The children, in need of some spending money of their own, looked for summer jobs. One by one, they went to work for Ward Eastman. In time, they were graduated from high school, each standing near the top of their class, and moved away to homes and families of their own. And that left Jerry and Larry alone again, each in his own side of the big house. Jerry wanted the door closed between the two living rooms, but Larry kept opening it.

As the twins grew older, Jerry became more and more of a recluse. He stopped going to the county seat and to church. "I've been going so many years, I've heard everything there is to hear and it's got so one preacher sounds the same as another," Jerry said. The folks who heard him say that said, "That sounds more like Larry than Jerry," but it wasn't. In time, he stopped going down to the village and relied on the telephone and the mail-order catalogue as the means of shopping for food, clothes, and the other staples he needed. At first, the delivery boy from the grocery store saw him when he brought the week's order, but one day he found a note that told him to leave the box on the back porch with the bill, which would be paid by mail. Then, he gave up calling in his order by 'phone; instead, he mailed his list for the following week along with his check for the groceries just left.

Larry—although he slowed down some with advancing age—remained the bon vivant and womanizer and stories of his excesses were still told in the local bar. While his escapades happened on a less-frequent basis than in earlier years, the locales of them got closer to home. That, of course, bothered Jerry and might have been what drove him into a deeper seclusion. When he told Larry he was old enough to know better, that made Larry mad. All of which served only to widen the rift between them. Finally, Larry said he was going to California where Maria and her family lived and he did. In parting, he told Jerry he didn't care what he did with the damn farm anyway.

But the farm too was getting older—Jerry had to put a new roof on the barn after a heavy snow caved in the old one and ruined half the hay still in the mows; the spring went dry and he had to drill a well, which meant added cost for a pump and the running of it to replace the gravity feed of the old system; the tractor finally gasped its last and he had to buy a new one.

As Jerry reached his mid-sixties, he realized that running the farm by himself no longer made any sense. Real estate taxes were going up every year and he had to pay them all. Even though the joint ownership of the property seemed to call for an equal split in the tax bill and a sharing of the other obligations, saying that and getting Larry to pay his half-share were two different things. It was time to sell the farm or, at least, as far as Jerry was concerned, his half or most of his half of it. He knew that some of those city folks would be interested in buying it. What Larry did with his half was his, or his children's, decision.

In order to work out a split of the property, they needed a surveyor, so Jerry called Ward Eastman, the obvious choice remembering the friendship that had existed between their fathers and, especially, the good experiences Larry's four children had enjoyed during the summers they worked for him. Ward was familiar with the terms of the will under which the twins shared the joint ownership and advised Jerry it was necessary that he and Larry agree on how the farm was to be divided into the two separate ownerships. Jerry knew this, but wasn't sure of Larry's whereabouts—the last he had heard of him was that day he left for California or, at least, that's where he said he was going.

He did, however, know where the four children were. They each remembered him as fondly as he remembered them and kept up a regular correspondence, periodically sending him pictures of their families as they grew, both in number and in years. They were the only friends he allowed in his reclusive world. He wrote each of them, told them of his decision to divide the farm so he could sell some of his half, and asked them all to come to the farm during July, bringing their father, wherever he was, if they knew. He told them a mutual understanding had to be reached, on the ground, as to where the dividing boundary line would be drawn.

Everybody came in early July all right, even Larry. But a few days after they arrived, Jerry Ford disappeared, never to be seen again. At least, that's what everyone thought as the days and the weeks went by.

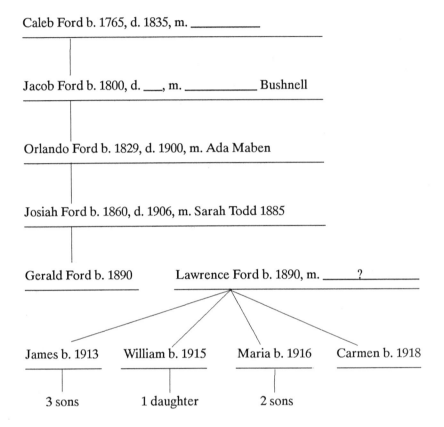

Caleb Ford b. 1765, d. 1835, m. _____

Jacob Ford b. 1800, d. ___, m. _____ Bushnell

Orlando Ford b. 1829, d. 1900, m. Ada Maben

Josiah Ford b. 1860, d. 1906, m. Sarah Todd 1885

Gerald Ford b. 1890   Lawrence Ford b. 1890, m. ____?_____

James b. 1913   William b. 1915   Maria b. 1916   Carmen b. 1918

3 sons   1 daughter   2 sons

Chapter 6

Murder at Big Rock

It WAS JERRY FORD ALL RIGHT, Ward Eastman was sure of that. However, that answered only one of numerous questions that would now be asked. The big rock wasn't teetering, but Ward was — he grabbed at the upper limbs of the maple tree and held on tightly to steady himself. It was a few minutes before he could gather himself together and step down off the tree trunk onto the flat surface of the rock.

He knew he shouldn't disturb anything, but he felt compelled to examine the area on top of the rock for some sign of what had happened those seven years ago. After all, Jerry Ford had been a friend of sorts, at least as much of a friend as Jerry would let himself be, and Ward wanted to know what fate had befallen him; not that knowing would do Jerry much good. Before moving away from the tree trunk, Ward slipped off his rucksack and took out the camera he always carried. He could, if nothing else, record on film the site as it first had greeted him.

The body or, more exactly, the skeleton, lay near the left or westerly side of the top of the rock just left of where the tree trunk lay. No flesh yet coated the bones, but remnants of clothing did. Jerry Ford had always worn the old-fashioned, bib overalls and the hooks at the end of the shoulder straps, with some tattered cloth attached, lay on the rib cage. The shoes were still on the feet — the soles were intact and the uppers were held together by remains of leather laces. Some shreds of cloth were visible under the skeleton. A pocket watch and a jackknife, both completely rusted, and some coins lay on the rock near the hip bone on the right side of the skeleton.

Ward took pictures of all this and the complete surface of the rock before he moved away from his stance beside the tree trunk. He walked around the rock, taking care not to move the leaves and other plant duff that nearly covered the entire surface of it. If he had not tripped over the eyebolt near the upper edge on the easterly side of the rock, he might not have seen it. He pulled the leaves away and saw it was a 3/4-of-an-inch bolt set in a hole that had been drilled in the rock so that only the looped head protruded. Who, how, why, and when it had been set were four questions Ward Eastman asked, but couldn't answer.

He moved more cautiously around the top of the rock after that, watching where he place his feet before he stepped. He found nothing else, however, although it was possible that some other remains were hidden under the leaves or the top of the tree up which he had climbed. He circled around the tree top, keeping as near to it as he could. He had no desire to walk next to the northerly edge of the big rock—it was a long drop from there to the bottom of the sheer ledge on which it rested.

The skeleton lay on its back with the skull up near the back or south-westerly corner of the rock. The right leg was bent at the knee with the right foot underneath the left shin bone. Both arms were raised with the hands resting on the rock, palmside up, one on each side of the skull. The position of the skeleton indicated that Jerry Ford had been backing toward the upper edge of the rock with arms raised as if to defend himself. Defend, indeed! It was then Ward noticed the markings on the front part of the skull over the left eye socket. Looking closer, he saw three distinct fracture points, each consisting of a circular depression about an inch or so in diameter, with cracks radiating outward from them. Jerry Ford hadn't died naturally then. He had been murdered, struck on the head with some object, probably a hammer. It had to have been a hammer, Ward concluded, nothing else, certainly not a stone, could have made such neat circles. A murder in the Catskills! Not unheard of, of course, but a rarity nonetheless.

Ward again methodically searched the entire surface of the big rock. It was obvious now that Jerry Ford had been murdered here, here on top of the rock. He had been trying to get away or, at least, was trying to protect his head when he was struck. That meant the murderer had also been on top of the rock; it wasn't as if he had been killed by a rifle bullet fired from on up the mountain slope. How had the two of them climbed the rock, especially Jerry, who was sixty-five when he disappeared? Probably, Ward thought, the eyebolt had something to do with it, but that answer only brought him back to the question of how the eyebolt had gotten there in the first place. He found no hammer, nor anything else. Jerry and his few possessions were all that were there.

Ward made his way back down the tree trunk and started a search of the ground nearby. He expected to find some remains of the rope that must have threaded through the eyebolt, but didn't. He didn't expect to find the hammer, he had already made up his mind that had been thrown off the rock and was somewhere in the scree at the bottom of the ledge. When he completed his search of the ground along the upper side of the big rock — he didn't find anything that didn't naturally belong there — he made his way easterly along the top of the ledge. He knew a gap existed about four hundred feet away. It was here the pipeline carrying water from the spring on up the mountain had run on its way to the reservoir that had once supplied water to the Ford house and farm buildings down on the flat. The spring had dried up years ago and he knew the pipes had then been taken up. He found the gap soon enough, climbed easily down it, turned westerly, and walked along the foot of the ledge.

When Ward reached a point under the big rock, he started another careful search among the rocks and stones that were scattered about. It was almost a lost cause, the hammer, or anything else for that matter, could easily have fallen between two rocks. Some of the gaps were big enough to break a leg he thought, if you happened to step in one. Nevertheless, he searched for over an hour, so sure he was the hammer would be there. It wasn't and neither did he find anything but more stones and rocks. "That makes the cheese more binding," he muttered to himself. Nothing was left then, but to climb on down the mountain and report his discovery to someone in authority.

The climb took a long time. Ward stopped frequently to ponder what he had found. More importantly, he wondered about what he hadn't found. He thought once about climbing back up to the big rock and making another search, but decided he wouldn't have any better success the second time around, so on down he went.

When he reached the farmhouse, all the Ford family was there, all except Larry that is, who had been too ill to make the trip from California. It was another gathering just like the one back in 1955 when they all had come to decide how to divide the land of the farm. After Jerry Ford had disappeared, that whole process had stopped — without him, no one else could make the final decision about his share. Now here they were again; they had been arriving over the past week or so. Each of the four children had come. Jim was with his wife, their three grown-up sons and their wives, and two little granddaughters. Bill was with his wife and their teen-aged daughter. Maria was alone, her marriage had ended in divorce some years before and her twin sons were in the middle of their internship. Carmen too was alone; she had vowed never to marry, she wanted no ties to hold her back from climbing in the remote mountain ranges of the world.

Ward was glad to see them all there; it was easier to tell his discovery just once before he called Roger Hurley, the Forest Ranger. As they listened intently, he watched their faces hoping to catch some clue from one who might not be as surprised as the rest, but didn't. All were genuinely shocked as he told them their Uncle Jerry had been murdered, but no one any less than the others as far as he could tell. He had already made up his mind one of them was guilty of the crime, but Larry Ford wasn't there and he was easily the prime suspect. However, he was jumping to conclusions and he really didn't have any reason to conclude anything except, who else would have wanted to kill Jerry Ford? Well! you damn fool, he thought, why would any of the family? None of them had gained anything. What did he know anyway? He was only a surveyor, not some smart detective; they only showed up in books. So he was back where he had begun the whole exercise.

Ward left the Fords and started for home, telling them he would notify the people to whom these things were supposed to be reported and suggested that none of them talk to anyone else until the State Police got in touch with them. He had no intention of notifying the State Police directly, but no need for them to know that. The last time he had anything to do with the State Police, he had decided that was the last time. That was when the little boy was lost over in the Peekamoose country. The forest rangers and the men from the survey crew ran the search while the troopers either walked along the road, careful not to dull the shine on their shoes, or went off in a patrol car, red light flashing, on their way for coffee and sandwiches. When the rangers found the boy, alive and well, after a three-day search, it was the troopers who got their pictures in the newspapers; the rangers and surveyors were not even mentioned.

Ward stopped at Roger Hurley's house on the way home. He found him in the garage tending to his truck, not surprisingly. Ward knew it had well over 100,000 miles on it, but the Albany Office had told Hurley that money was short in this year's budget and he had to make it run another year. Hell too! Ward thought to himself; next year they'd tell Hurley the same thing while all the troopers on the mountaintop got new cars. Hurley was glad when told the search was finally over — he had been involved in trying to find some trace of Jerry Ford back in 1955 and never was satisfied that as much had been done as should have been. He asked Ward to meet him at daybreak at the Ford farm. It was dark now and, since Jerry had been on the rock for seven years, they were sure another night wouldn't make much difference. In the meantime, Hurley agreed to notify the State Police, the sheriff, the coroner, and any others who needed to know.

It was a long evening. Of course, Ward told Betty of the events of the day, how he had found the body, or skeleton, the reactions of the various Fords, and his visit with Ranger Hurley. After supper, he lit his pipe — finally — leaned his head against the back of the chair, closed his eyes, and thought back to those days in 1955 when Jerry Ford had disappeared.

Jerry had gotten in touch with him by letter in early June of that year. By that time, Jerry had told the telephone company (by letter) to come and pick up their damn 'phone. If he wasn't going to use it — and he wasn't — he didn't want it around ringing all the time and bothering him. Besides that, he was getting sick and tired of receiving a bill every month for something he didn't need. Since he hadn't paid the bill for six months, the telephone company was only too glad to remove the 'phone. When the serviceman arrived, he found it sitting on the back step together with the drop wire, that had run from the corner of the house out to the pole beside the road, wound neatly in a loop beside it.

The letter to Ward was written in a fine, flowing, elegant hand reminding him of the way his mother and father had written. Jerry wrote, in plain English, that he needed to see him about a business matter and expected Ward to call at his house at 10:00 AM on Saturday next. Nothing more was written, nor did it need to be.

Ward arrived at Jerry's house at the appointed time, not five minutes early or five minutes late; he had dealt with Jerry before and knew when he said ten o'clock in the morning, that's what he meant. It was during that meeting that Ward had advised him it would be necessary for all the parties interested in the division of the farm to agree or a survey would be wasted. Since Jerry didn't know for sure where Larry was or even if he was still alive, Ward suggested that at least one of the children must know his whereabouts. Jerry said if Larry did show up, he wouldn't trust him. He asked Ward to lend him a one-chain tape and a hand compass so he could measure up some of the land before Larry came — if he really did come, that is. That way maybe he could once get the best of Larry, he said. Even though Ward didn't think that was a fair way to go about it, he did drop off an extra chain and compass the next time he passed through South Branch.

So it was that the four children came in July. Larry was with Maria and her twin sons, then aged sixteen. Her husband had left some years before and she had somehow divorced him in abstentia since she or no one else could locate him. It was somewhat of a turnabout to hear Larry condemn the long-gone husband for not fulfilling his family obligations.

Surprisingly, Jerry, Larry, and the four children had no trouble agreeing how the property was to be split. Larry had mellowed somewhat with time or, perhaps, from having been apart from Jerry for so long. Jerry became more sociable when the children arrived and they spent hours talking about their years growing up under his watchful eye while their father roamed the countryside in search of the good times. Even Larry laughed at that, saying he knew Jerry would be a far better father than he, so he had just given him the opportunity.

In the end, the decision was that the farm would be split into three parts instead of two. A ten-acre parcel was to be laid out along the town road that crossed the farm on its way up the valley. The north boundary was to run along the stream and the parcel was to include the house and all the other buildings. Jerry was to have the use of this land and the buildings on it for the rest of his life. At his death, it was to go to Larry or, in the event of his prior death, to the four children jointly. The remainder of the farm was to be split into two parts with the dividing line to run from the mid-point on the back line of the ten-acre parcel (which would be near the center of the north end of the farm because that's where the house was) up the mountain to the big rock, and pivot at that point so the line, when it intersected the southerly line of the total property, split the remainder farm into two equal parts. Jerry was to get the westerly half and Larry was to get the easterly half and each could then do what he wanted with his part. It sounded complicated, but it wasn't. It was a straight-forward surveying exercise with the only problem being the time-consuming task of traversing the long lines up and down the mountain. Ward asked the four children if they wanted to take another turn at swinging an ax for the summer, but all declined. Those days were over each thought, and would rather that Ward's regular crew took care of the necessary bullwork. Ward agreed to start the survey as soon as he completed the one he was then working on and expected that would be about the third week in July. But the survey was never started. Jerry Ford disappeared on the Friday before that.

The days prior had not been unusual, at least as far as any of the Fords could tell. Jerry had acted the same or, if anything, more open and friendly as each day of their visit went by. He spent every evening in the library, quietly reading book after book from his father's collection, but they thought nothing about that although Jerry hadn't been much of a reader before. No time for it then, he had said. During the day, he went about the never-ending tasks needed to keep the farm running. However, those were not as demanding as they once had been because the numbers of farm animals had been cut back over the years as Jerry had found it more and more difficult to keep up. Still, the daily chores remained — while lesser in scope, the number of them seemed not to have decreased.

On the Thursday evening all the Fords, including Larry, but excepting Jerry, had gone to Hunter to the movies — some shoot-'em-up western in which Jerry had absolutely no interest and besides, he said, he didn't want to be around all those people. They had left him reading in the library. When they returned home, all the lights were off except one outside, over the back door, that Jerry had left on for them. Jerry's pick-up truck was parked out beside the barn where he always left it. They assumed he had gone to bed in his side of the house.

In the morning, Bill was the first up and noticed Jerry's truck was gone. He thought no more about it, assuming Jerry had gone to town for something. However, later on someone (Ward couldn't recall which one of them it had been) noticed the three cows (all that were left on the farm) standing in the lot by the barn door. They hadn't been milked and, then, they realized the chickens hadn't been fed or the eggs collected. All that was unusual; Jerry was the methodical one of the family, always doing the farm chores and every other daily task at a certain time each day without fail, regardless

52

of the weather or his state of health. Surely, some emergency had claimed his attention that morning. However, they weren't overly worried, although puzzled that Jerry had left no note of explanation. Between them, they took care of the morning farm chores and each went on with his or her plans for the day.

Ward couldn't recall where each had gone, but he did remember that all of the younger generation had left before anyone else was out of bed (except for Jerry as their testimony later noted, his pick-up truck was already gone when they first went out). They had caught the milk truck on its way up the valley and spent the rest of the day hiking to the fire tower on Hunter Mountain and walking most of the way back to the farm. Ward also remembered that Larry and each of his four children had individually left the farm as soon as the chores had been taken care of and hadn't returned until suppertime. Bill's wife and Jim's had driven to Albany and spent the day shopping there — they were the last to arrive back at the farm. Jerry hadn't yet returned, nor had he by the following morning.

Finally, by the middle of the next day (Saturday), they decided something had happened to Jerry and someone should be called. Bill had driven down to the village and called the State Police on the one pay telephone there (on the side of the grocery store). A little later, a trooper arrived at the farm and listened to their story. He seemed not to be overly concerned and advised the family not to make something big out of what he had found was a common occurrence. People were always disappearing for a day or two, but they usually came back. He was sure Jerry would show up the next day or the day after. Still, he took down a description of the pick-up truck and the license number (which, luckily, one of the young lads remembered) and said he would have his barracks put out a bulletin for all troopers to be on the lookout for it.

But Jerry didn't come back the next day or the day after. He wasn't back three week later when a trooper came to tell them the truck had been found in the parking lot at the railroad station in Hudson, some thirty-five miles away over the Rip Van Winkle bridge across the Hudson River from Catskill. It was empty, nothing in the back or nothing in the cab to indicate what had happened; no clothes, no suitcase, nothing that didn't belong there. The doors were locked and the keys were not in the ignition or anywhere in the truck.

Thereafter, the State Police had centered their efforts on questioning people who regularly rode the trains that ran through Hudson. They stationed a trooper in the parking lot for a couple of weeks and he questioned everyone who used the lot. Had they seen the truck? When had they first noticed it? Had it been there continuously from the time they had first seen it? Had they seen anyone around the truck? Had it been moved — was it parked in the same place as when first seen? Other troopers boarded the various trains that stopped at Hudson and questioned the passengers, showing them a picture of Jerry Ford, but no one remembered seeing him. No one, not even the employees at the station had noticed anything out-of-the-ordinary about the truck, or given any attention to it. It was like any other vehicle left in the parking lot; it just seemed to be there.

After a couple of months, the whole incident of the disappearance was nearly forgotten. The Ford family all went back to their homes and daily lives. Bill had stayed on the longest. He was a teacher somewhere in Pennsylvania and delayed his return home until just before school started. While there at South Branch, he had taken care of the farm, but finally made arrangements with the Schermerhorns next door to add the animals to their livestock herds and to watch over the buildings and land of the farm.

It was not as if the Catskills hadn't seen some strange deaths before and even a murder or two. Ward had been involved in a couple of these, one being the young climber from the village, who had fallen from the ledge just under the big rock. The climber's friend had rushed down the mountain with the sad story and Ward had been one of the group, along with Ranger Hurley, that climbed the mountain to bring the body down.

And Ward and his survey crew had been part of the massive effort in 1940 that had searched for the deer hunter from Long Island who had disappeared on up the valley. His companions had let him off beside the road early in the morning with the understanding that he would hunt the slopes of Evergreen Mountain on the north side of the valley and meet them at the same spot along the roadside at dusk. He didn't show up that evening and, when he wasn't heard from by noon the following day, his friends reported his disappearance to Dan Raines, the Forest Ranger who had preceded Hurley in the area. The search went on for about three weeks, but no trace of the hunter was ever turned up. A story made the rounds some months later that the hunter had been having marital problems and simply walked over the mountain to Hunter where his lady friend was waiting and they rode off into the sunset as it were, never to be seen again. How much truth that story held, Ward wondered, because it had never been confirmed one way or the other as far as he knew.

Perhaps the strangest death was that of Brazil Pelham, who lived near the head of the valley back about the turn of the century. Pelham hung himself and, while that was strange enough, the reason for it was stranger still. It seems, so the story goes, that Pelham had been getting "The Windham Journal," the local newspaper, in the mail for some length of time although he had never subscribed to it. Finally, the newspaper realized its error and sent Pelham a bill for those years he had been receiving it. Pelham was overwhelmed by the bill itself and, especially, the amount of it and went out to the barn and hung himself from the main beam in the hay mow.

A couple of murders, equally odd, had occurred about the same period of time. One of these was relatively far away, but Ward remembered it because he had heard his father speak of it a number of times. The murder victim was the Huntington's caretaker, a friend of Josiah Ford's from the time he worked on their estate. His body was found in the den of the Huntington lodge one December morning, shot through the head. The speculation was he had surprised a burglar in the act. Ward couldn't remember if anything had actually been stolen or if the murderer had been caught and he hadn't ever thought to ask Jerry Ford about the incident.

The other murder took place up the valley of the South Branch and involved a boundary line and a land surveyor or, at least, a pseudo-land surveyor. Jim Black had laid out the boundary lines of his farm (in the wrong place, as Ward found out for himself years later when he surveyed the back line of it where it ran along the State land). His neighbor, Pardee Shoemaker, tried to explain to Black where the line between their properties really was and pointed out that Black's survey had taken a strip of land off the Shoemaker farm. Black insisted his survey was right and warned Shoemaker that if he stepped over the surveyed line he would be trespassing and he, Black, would shoot him. Well, they both did; that is, Shoemaker crossed the line to claim the land he felt was rightfully his and Black shot him. The court took a dim view of that extreme action — whether or not the survey was correct wasn't a factor — and Black spent the rest of his life in the State penitentiary.

All that, however, was then and now is now, thought Ward Eastman as he knocked the ashes out of his cold pipe and climbed the stairs to bed. Tomorrow might bring some answers — more than likely, it would bring only more questions.

THIS INDENTURE, made the Twenty-Second day of January, Nineteen Hundred and Six BETWEEN Colonel Jonathan Craig of Deep Notch House in the Town of Lexington, County of Greene, and State of New York, party of the first part, and Josiah Ford of South Branch in the Town, County, and State aforesaid, party of the second part,

Witnesseth, that the party of the first part, in consideration of One Dollar lawful money of the United States, paid by the party of the second part and other good and valuable consideration, does hereby remise, release, and quitclaim unto the party of the second part, his heirs and assigns forever, ALL that certain piece or parcel of land, and the buildings thereon, lying and being in the town, county, and state aforesaid and being a part of the unallotted part of Great Lot 21 of the Hardenburgh Patent bounded and described as follows; **Beginning** at a point in the center of the South Branch where the same is intersected by the division line between said Great Lot 21 and Great Lot 22 of said Hardenburgh Patent and runs thence South thirty eight degrees and fifteen minutes West along said division line and lands of one Willisam Schermerhorn being marked partly by a stone wall a distance of eighty seven chains, seventy five links to a pile of stones; thence North fifty two degrees West along the line of lands of the party of the first part herein a distance of thirty six chains, sixty links to a pile of stones; thence North 38 degrees and 15 minutes East along the line of said lands of the party of the first part and lands formerly of Aaron Bushnell this last being along a stone wall a distance of eighty nine chains and twenty links to the center of the South Branch aforesaid; thence southeasterly up and along the center of the said South Branch a distance of about 37 chains to the place of beginning; **Containing** three hundred twenty three acres. **Further** confirming the right of the party of the second part to take one half of the water from the Musgrave spring, so-called, situate on lands of the party of the first part aforesaid and the right to go upon said lands to locate, lay, maintain, repair, and replace a pipeline or some other device to carry such water beginning at said Musgrave spring and running northeasterly to and into lands of the party of the second part herein and as described hereinabove. **Excepting and reserving** the rights of the public and the Town of Lexington in and to the road that crosses the northerly part of the hereinabove described farm.

AND INTENDING to convey those same lands and rights that were heretofore conveyed by Chauncey Musgrave to Caleb Ford by deed dated the sixteenth day of January, 1802.

Together with the appurtenances and all the estate and rights of the party of the first part in and to said premises.

To have and to hold the premises herein granted unto the party of the second part, his heirs and assigns forever.

In Witness Whereof, the party of the first part has hereunto set his hand and seal the day and year first above written.

Chapter 7

Investigation

MORNING CAME EARLY to Ward Eastman — he had not slept well, lying awake most of the night going over and over the events of the day before and those he could remember from seven years ago. It was all for nothing; everything still seemed a jumble and even more so when the picture of Jerry Ford's skeleton flashed across the lids of his closed eyes. Still, he knew that in time the facts would sort themselves out and he would remember whatever it was that lurked in the back of his mind nagging at him. He had forgotten something and, when he remembered it, he knew he would have the answer to one of the questions, whichever one it was would have to wait until then. This was not a new experience for him. Many times before, when starting a survey, the complicated deeds that made up the chains of title to the property he was surveying and to the properties adjoining seemed as confusing and just as unlikely of resolution. All of a sudden, when he least expected it and usually when he was involved in or thinking about some other subject, the way out of the maze would become clear and the pieces of the deeds would fit together. He hoped such would be the case with the murder of Jerry Ford, but he wondered if he had yet read all the deeds.

When he arrived at the Ford farm at daybreak, he found Roger Hurley already there. A number of his fellow Forest Rangers were with him and they stood about talking, their trucks parked in the open space in front of the barn. It was amazing, Ward thought, just how old and worn out all the trucks were, but still running smoothly, babied along by the rangers, who each knew that the chance of the State replacing the trucks anytime soon was remote at best.

The early hour turned out to be wasted effort. Hurley had reported Ward's find to the State Police and was told to wait at the farmhouse until the troopers and other law enforcement officials got there to take charge of the investigation. It was some two hours later before they showed up. By then, the Fords were up and about and brought out cups of hot coffee to Ward and the rangers as they waited, pacing up and down the back yard, anxious to get started. The troopers finally arrived, driving shiny and new vehicles, accompanied by someone from the county sheriff's office and a representative of the county coroner. Some looked like they hadn't walked much in years and then no farther than from the parking lot into the local restaurant. It was going to be a long trek up the mountain, Ward thought, and not a very pleasant one either as dreary clouds thickened overhead and a drizzle of rain began to fall. It was a good day to be involved in a murder.

It was, indeed, a long climb. Rests along the way were frequent as one member or another of the "official" group called a halt. The moss and lichens covering the rocks underfoot turned slippery as the rain continued to fall and the smooth soles on the shoes of many of the party found no firm traction as they climbed. Slips and falls were frequent and Hurley once mumbled to the ranger carrying the stretcher, "Looks like we should have brought some extra of those; we may have to carry more than a skeleton off this mountain."

The small ledge at the end of the stone wall and the steepening slope above it stopped the man from the coroner's office. He announced he would return to the farmhouse and wait until the skeleton was brought there for his examination. He was wet through by then, not having brought any foul-weather gear along. He grumbled as he turned about and started downhill; his first step was an uncontrolled slide across the slanted rock on which he was standing at the time. Hurley shook his head in disbelief and turned his fellow rangers uphill.

At the steep rift in the high ledge, the chief investigator, a plainclothes-man named Bryan, in charge of the contingent of State Police told off three of the troopers and instructed them to proceed left along the foot of the ledge until they were beneath the big rock and to search for anything that might have fallen or been thrown there and could have some connection to the murder. As the three looked doubtfully along the rough ground ahead of them, Hurley suggested that one of the Forest Rangers go along to guide them to the location under the big rock. The investigator agreed and one of the rangers took the lead of the group.

The rest of the Forest Rangers and police assemblage followed Ward up the cleft in the ledge, moving from sapling to sapling for support as they went. The loosened soil quickly turned to slippery mud as one by one they climbed the steep slope. The footing was firmer along the top of the ledge and they were soon in sight of the big rock as it loomed through the misty rain. Here Bryan halted the procession and moved forward along it until he reached Ward and Hurley at the front. He asked Ward to lead along the route he had first followed to reach the base of the tree leaning against the big rock. The three of them, together with the man from the sheriff's office and a couple of troopers — one of them being a photographer — were to walk this track and climb the tree to the top of the rock. This would keep the disturbance to the surrounding area to a minimum although all agreed that, after all these years, it probably didn't make much difference.

The other troopers and Forest Rangers were detailed to make a thorough search around the big rock and of much of the area at the top of the ledge. They formed in a line with the end man being next to the ledge and the others spread out above him leaving about a three-foot space between one man and the next. Once so positioned, they began to slowly work their way to and around the big rock. Each man carefully turned over the leaves and twigs in his path as he went, methodically checking each square inch of ground for any clue or remains of the events of those seven long years ago.

In the meantime, Ward led Bryan, Hurley, and the others back westerly along the top of the ledge and then southerly in a big loop around the area being searched by the troopers and rangers to reach the route he had followed the day before. They turned northerly along this track and walked downhill to the base of the fallen tree. Here Bryan directed the trooper/photographer to go first up the tree and take photographs of the top of the big rock before it was further disturbed by those following. Ward could hear the clicking of the camera and see the flash of the bulbs as he went about his work. As they waited, the rain stopped and a few patches of blue began to show through the gray overhead — Ward and Hurley removed their raingear and stuffed it into the rucksacks each carried.

When the photographer called down that he was finished, the others, one by one, made their way up the slippery trunk of the leaning tree. Although Ward knew the picture that would greet him as he topped the edge of the rock, he was startled nonetheless to again see the bleached skeleton and the hollow eyes of the skull staring at him. All stood still and silent for a few minutes as they took in the scene. Bryan removed a small loose-leaf notebook from the pouch he carried and drew a sketch outlining the rock and noting where the body or skeleton lay. He asked Ward and Hurley to make some measurements with a cloth tape he had brought along so the sketch could be dimensioned. He then made a series of written notes describing his impressions, the position of the skeleton, and the indentations in the skull.

All that done, they moved the skeleton, placing it in a large canvas bag Hurley had borrowed from the undertaker in Hunter the evening before. He and Ward, with help from a couple of the rangers on the ground, maneuvered the bag down the tree trunk. The skeleton seemed surprisingly light to Ward, he still thought of it as the Jerry Ford he had once known and expected it to be the same as if it was his body. The rangers placed the bag on the stretcher they had brought and rejoined the line of men slowly working their way over the ground next to the big rock.

Ward and Hurley reclimbed the tree and joined Bryan and the others in a similar slow, methodical search of the top of the rock. They didn't find much beyond what Ward had seen the day before — the photographer took a couple of close-up shots of the eyebolt set in the drill hole near the southeasterly corner of the rock surface. He also took pictures of the pocket watch, jackknife, and loose change as they lay on the now bare surface of the rock. When Bryan picked up the watch to put it in a small leather sack he carried, they saw that a key lay under it. The photographer took some pictures of it before Bryan moved it. It was a large key, obviously an old one, and looked like some of the so-called antique keys Ward had seen at flea markets. The word"Yale" was inscribed in a semicircle around the upper edge of the flat part of the key. They all speculated that it probably fit a padlock of some early vintage, but where it was was another mystery.

Except for some metal buttons that had been part of the overalls Jerry Ford had worn and some shreds of cloth, they found nothing else. They moved every leaf and carefully looked at every inch of the rock's surface. It was as if Jerry Ford was the only other person who had ever been there. Obviously that wasn't so, but whomever else had once been on top of the rock had left no sign.

The searchers on the ground at the top of the ledge had also drawn a blank. A shouted conversation with the group at the bottom of the ledge determined that they had had no better success. All that remained of Jerry Ford and those moments of seven years before were his skeleton and what he had carried there in his pockets. Even all that was commonplace except for the key. Rather than finding any clue to help solve the mystery of what had happened then, the key only added another question to the list of the many seeking answers.

By this time, it was early afternoon. The sun had broken through the clouds and a slight breeze had gradually dried the forest growth. The unproductive, but necessary, search over, nothing remained but to descend the mountain, bearing the grisly remains of the past with them.

The climb was slow and quiet. The group from the bottom of the ledge was waiting at the rift when the upper group made their way down it. All were silent as they descended. It was as if each of them was going over and over what he had seen, trying to make things fit with what they knew about the disappearance and investigation of seven years ago. Nothing did, however. As Ward had already decided, that was then and now was now. Still, he thought, the two times had to be brought together. When they were, the identity of the one person who could bridge that gap of years would be known and Jerry Ford's murderer would have a name. Maybe, also, Ward hoped, they would find the lock that damn key would open.

The procession finally reached the area of the farm buildings. The Ford family members gathered about as the coroner, who had arrived during the morning, took charge of the canvas bag and the remains in it. It was a sad end to a person who had been such a vital part of their lives. Still, it was better that he would no longer remain exposed to the weather and the changing seasons. Knowing Jerry Ford, however, he probably would have rested just as easy, or easier, up there on his own land surrounded by the hills he loved.

Bryan thanked Ward and Hurley and the Forest Rangers for their help. The standard "we couldn't have done it without you" didn't sound as hollow as it might have. Even Ward, cynical as he was when it came to the State Police, had to acknowledge that the troopers had not held back or shirked the duties assigned to them. Some would sleep soundly tonight, he thought; the climb up and down must have been difficult, but they had "kept up" and hadn't complained. "If only I had them on a survey crew for about six months, I could turn them into something worthwhile," he muttered to himself.

As he was leaving, Bryan told the Fords he would be back the next day to again talk with them about what they remembered from the day Jerry Ford had disappeared and the days leading up to it. He also asked Ward and Hurley to keep themselves available over the next week or so as he would probably want to discuss various aspects about then and now with them. Ward and Hurley left soon after and the Fords were then alone to deal again with a family tragedy they had dealt with once before.

Ward Eastman spent another restless night, waking a number of times during the hours after midnight. When he awoke for the last time early in the morning, he decided he might just as well get up. As he sat in the kitchen drinking his first cup of coffee, he scolded himself for getting so wound up in something that wasn't really any of his business. Still, it was. He had, after all, been the one who had found Jerry Ford and he had yet a nagging feeling that he was more involved than he knew. Finally, he closed his mind to it all and left for the County Clerk's Office in Kingston, where he had to spend at least one whole day running down deeds in preparation for an extensive survey over in Denning.

On the Thursday evening following, Ward had a telephone call from Bryan of the State Police asking if he could come to the barracks in Leeds to give a statement about his finding of the skeleton. Although the request was stated as a question, it was still a request that one could hardly refuse, so Ward set aside his plans for the next day. He didn't really mind as much as he made out when he complained to Betty about the thoughtlessness of those damn troopers anyway. He had not given much thought to the Ford business over the past couple of days and, now that his mind was clear of it, perhaps he would be better able to sort things out.

Bryan greeted him cordially and Ward smiled back at him in spite of himself as they shook hands. A police stenographer was called in and Bryan asked Ward to describe, in his own words, the circumstances of why he was on the mountain in the first place, why he had gone to the big rock, and what he had found when he got to the top of it. It took about an hour to go over it all beginning seven years earlier when Jerry Ford had asked him to survey the farm and ending when he stopped at Roger Hurley's place on the way home to report his discovery.

As they waited in the office while the stenographer went out to type the statement, Bryan subtly began a series of questions about the individuals of the Ford family. It soon became obvious that he suspected one of them as being the murderer, but didn't know which one or what had been the motive. Ward was sure he hadn't been of much help when the questions ended, but had to agree that Bryan's sense was sound. Ward had known all of the Fords over the years and the Ford children had worked for him in their formative years when their character flaws would have been the most noticeable. But Ward had nothing out of the ordinary to report. All four of the children had their individual traits, but each had been dependable, hard-working, agreeable, and interested in what they were doing. Larry Ford was another matter entirely, but Ward added nothing to the information Bryan already had about him.

Ward thought it only fair to ask Bryan about his investigation and what, if any, determinations he had been able to make. While Bryan was open in his response, it turned out he hadn't made much progress toward any conclusions. All of the Fords except, of course, Larry, who was in a nursing home in California, had been subjected to a number of sessions of probing questioning. And even Larry hadn't been excluded — the Sheriff of Sutter County had questioned him in the nursing home in Yuba City and had telephoned his report to Bryan. Although memories had faded a bit in the seven-year interval, everyone's story matched with those of that time and with each other's. The blank wall of 1955 was just as blank now, Bryan admitted.

Jerry Ford's body or, more correctly, remains were released by the coroner and the State Police to the family on the next Monday and the funeral was scheduled for Wednesday. The coroner's report, which Bryan had at the time of his interview with Ward, stated that death had resulted from multiple blows to the head, which, of course, didn't tell Ward anything he didn't know. The dentist in Tannersville positively identified the skeleton as that of Jerry Ford through his records of the dental work he had done for Jerry over the years. That also wasn't any new information to Ward. Who else could it have been? However, it was good to have confirmation of the fact even though nobody much doubted who the skeleton was.

Ward was asked to be one of the bearers at the funeral along with Roger Hurley; Russ Schermerhorn, the farmer next door; and three other one-time farmer friends of Jerry's from up the valley. The casket was lighter than others Ward had helped carry and, why not, this one didn't have much in it. Jerry was buried in the family plot, next to the graves of his mother and father, in the old cemetery on the little bluff in back of the settlement of South Branch. It was a beautiful day, but cooler than usual for the middle of July, and the birds sang from the trees overhead. The graveside service was interrupted now and then by the roar of tractor-trailer trucks as they sped around the wide, sweeping turn at the foot of the bluff on their way off the steep decline of the road through Deep Notch. Ward wondered again if Jerry Ford hadn't rested more peaceably back on the top of the big rock and was a little sorry he had ever found him.

Ward and all the others attending the funeral were, as tradition in the valley held, invited back to the Ford farm for refreshments after the service was concluded. He readily accepted, looking at the get-together as a good opportunity to do some questioning of his own. He had made up his mind to conduct an investigation of the murder, unofficial, of course, after he realized the State Police were making little or no headway in the one they were conducting. He intended to talk separately to each of the members of the family and he needed to do it quickly as he had heard some of them were going to leave for their own homes over the next few days. He had no plan of action beyond that and wasn't even sure what questions to ask or who to ask them of.

In mid-afternoon, once Ward had exchanged the usual pleasantries and sympathies with those who had come to the farmhouse and he had finished the food piled on his paper plate from the buffet he was sure Maria had prepared, he sought out the Ford brothers and sisters. He first spotted Carmen off across the field on the east side of the house, leaning against the fence, looking absently at the horses in the pasture of the Schermerhorn farm next door.

Carmen was the youngest of the Ford children; she had been only eight when Larry Ford brought the four of them back to the farm. That had been in 1926, which would have made her 37 at the time Jerry disappeared and 44 now. Being the youngest, she had been the last to spend her teenage summers working for Ward Eastman. He remembered her fondly. She had been an energetic person, not at all reluctant to wade through streams and swamps, always ready to tackle whatever was assigned to her including swinging an ax all day long—although cursing every step of the way as she worked through the ten-foot high laurel brush on that survey on Mt. Tobias up out of Wittenberg. She did, however, have a temper. More than once, when something hit her just the wrong way at the wrong time, she threw down her ax at the end of the day and said she would never return. The next morning she would be ready for work, mutter an "I'm sorry" as she climbed in the car when Ward or someone else picked her up, and sat there saying nothing until they reached the survey site. She also could not pass by a large boulder or a ledge without climbing it or making a good try at it. Ward was not surprised when, after high school, Carmen lit out for Colorado and the high peaks of the Rocky Mountains. Now and then, he read about her exploits in some of the outdoor magazines he subscribed to. Most of the articles began "Carmen Ford became the first woman to climb Mt. so-and-so. . . ."

Carmen looked up as Ward approached. "Are you sad?" he asked.

"No, not sad. Mad would be more like it. Mad at myself, because I never took the time to thank Uncle Jerry for all he did for me. You know, it wasn't easy growing up as the youngest of four children almost literally left on a doorstep. But it would have been a lot harder if Uncle Jerry hadn't watched out for me and taken my side when the other three picked on me. Do you remember all those times I quit working for you and swore I'd never come back?" Ward nodded in answer. "Well, he always seemed to know when I'd done that. He'd sit me down after supper and tell me I owed it to you not to quit because you were doing me a favor by giving me a job in the first place. He'd tell me I had to learn to be a responsible person and sometimes that meant doing something I didn't like. In the morning, he would see that I was up at the usual time, packed my lunch, and stood on the back step to make sure I got in the car when it came to pick me up. I kind of resented all that then, but years later, when I was out on my own, I remembered all those lectures, and based a lot of decisions — correct ones — on them. And I never really told him that.

"The troopers who talked to me said that you found the eyebolt set in the top of the big rock," Carmen went on. Ward nodded again and settled against the fence to listen — this questioning was turning out to be more of a monologue, which was fine with him.

"Uncle Jerry and I put that there," Carmen said. "I was interested in climbing for as far back as I can remember. My father says I climbed every chair and table in our apartment long before I could walk. When we came to the farm, it was like going to Heaven. I climbed every tree around, walked all the beams in the barn, and, once, went up one side of the barn, across the peak, and down the opposite side. It was then Uncle Jerry said I had to learn how to rappel, fix belay points, and set anchors and runners. In other words, he said, I had to learn how to correctly do the things I was trying to do before I fell off something and killed myself and then I wouldn't be much good to anybody, not that he really cared mind you. I didn't even know what

64

he was talking about with some of those terms, but he had bought a handbook on climbing somewhere and told me to read and study it until I understood how to do all the maneuvers and techniques described in it.

"I started rappelling out of the upper window of the barn, looping a rope over one of the beams, and coming down the double rope along the outside wall. After I got really good at it, Uncle Jerry said it was time we tried some real climbing. A few mornings later — I remember it was a sunny, blue-sky day just like this one — he handed me a new rucksack loaded with hardware, my lunch, and a water jug, all mine to keep, he said, except the lunch, which I could eat when the time came. I was thrilled; it was just like Christmas. Uncle Jerry had a filled rucksack of his own and a coil of rope that he slung over his shoulder.

"I didn't know where we were going when we started up the mountain, but the higher we climbed, the more I was sure we were heading for the high ledge and the big rock. We climbed up that cleft in the ledge and went easterly until we reached the rock. 'Well, here we are,' he said. 'I don't think anyone has ever climbed this rock before, but we're going to.' We took off our sacks and he dumped his out. It held a number of flat, thin, metal wedges about two inches wide and six inches long, about 1/4 of an inch thick at one end and tapered to an edge at the other. 'I made these out of the leaves of an old car spring,' he told me. 'I don't know if they have a name, or if they'll work the way I think they ought to, but we'll give it a try.'

"We went to the upper side of the big rock and Uncle Jerry pointed out the thin, horizontal cracks that crisscrossed its surface. He took the hammer he had brought in his sack and drove one of the wedges into a crack about three feet up the rock. When it stuck out about four inches, he told me I could tell it was solid because of the firm ringing sound it made when he hit it with the hammer. He stepped up on that wedge and balanced on it with one foot while he drove in another higher up. He kept setting those wedges until he had a regular ladder to the top. I was so surprised and told him I didn't know he could climb. He said, 'I didn't know I could either, but I thought I'd better find out before you got yourself stuck on some cliff or another and I had to come and get you down.'

"He sat down on top of the big rock, braced himself, took the coil of rope, threw one end of it down, told me to tie on the way we had practiced, and climb up the wedges. He kept the rope taut as I climbed, just the way the handbook said to do when a climber was on belay. Then he said we were going to fix a point in the top of the rock so I would have something solid to anchor to while I rappelled down the high ledge. He took a rock drill out of his sack and, taking turns with the hammer, we drilled a hole in the rock. When we had it about three inches deep, he took an eyebolt from his sack, and pounded it, a tight fit, into the hole. He then took the long rope, threaded it through the eye in the bolt, and threw the doubled rope over

65

the rock so that it hung down the ledge. He looked over the edge of the big rock to make sure that the rope reached the bottom, turned to me and said, 'Now, see if you can go down that.'

"That was the first real rappel I ever did and it was exciting. Whenever I do a rappel now, I always remember that first one. But that wasn't all the surprises he had in store for that day. When I reached the scree at the bottom of the ledge and was off the rope, he pulled up one end leaving a single strand of it hanging down. He hollared for me to tie on the end of the rope and climb the ledge while he protected me by a belay through the eyebolt. I climbed it all right although it took me a long time. I slipped more than once and I think I wet my pants when I came off a hold near the top, but I needn't have worried because Uncle Jerry kept the rope tight all the while I climbed.

"We made many a trip to the big rock. I learned how to tie a Prusik knot and climb up the rope, did pendulum swings across the face of the ledge, and climbed routes all over it, up, down, and across, while belayed from that eyebolt by Uncle Jerry, patient as ever no matter what I wanted to try. He told me to keep our climbing a secret between us. 'Everybody around here thinks I'm odd now, no need to give 'em a real reason to think so.'

"I should have realized he might be up there, but I never gave it a thought. With his truck gone, I supposed he had driven to Hunter, or Catskill, or someplace. The big rock never entered my mind. I should have thought of it. I might have been able to help him."

It had been a long story and a startling one. Odd! Indeed, the townspeople would have through Jerry Ford really was crazy if they had known about him climbing up and down that big rock and hanging over the high ledge. While he now knew how Jerry had gotten to the top of the big rock, Ward didn't know much else except, perhaps, the hammer he used to drive the metal wedges into the cracks in the rock might have been what the murderer used to hit Jerry in the head. But where was the hammer and where, for that matter, were the wedges? He was sure they weren't still in the rock. Or were they? He hadn't noticed them, but he hadn't known to look for them either.

"How many of those wedges did you and Jerry use to climb up the big rock?" Ward finally asked.

Carmen pondered a minute before replying. "It's been such a long time, I can't really remember. Must be ten or so."

"Did you leave them in the cracks once they were set?"

"Oh, no. Uncle Jerry always took them out each time we used them. It took only a few sideways taps on each one to loosen it enough so it could be pulled out. He said if we left them in the rock, someone would surely come along, climb up on top, and fall over the ledge. He kept them in his rucksack which he hung on a hook in the corner of the workshop, but it's not there now and I can't find the wedges either. I looked that evening after you told us you had found him. But that may not mean anything because I haven't seen or looked for them or the rucksack since I first left the farm years ago."

"What did you do the day Jerry disappeared in 1955?" Ward then asked.

"You sound like the police now," Carmen answered. "They asked me that then and again the other day. I went climbing on the ledges in the Stony Clove Notch next to Devil's Tombstone Campsite. I think I'm the first one who climbed them. Or, at least, I never say any sign that anyone else had ever been there. I left right after we finished taking care of the farm animals that morning. I drove over on one of those motor scooters that were all the rage then. Bill had rented a bunch of them somewhere so we each would have a way to get around while we were here at the farm. I hid it in the woods down the old railroad grade, chained and padlocked fast to a tree. I climbed all day, did a number of routes on the cliffs, and didn't get back to the farm until supper time."

"Was anyone with you during the day or did anyone see you or you them?"

Carmen laughed, "You really do sound like the police. No. I was alone all day and saw only the cars that drove by on Route 214 way down under the ledges. I don't think anyone ever looked up to where I was."

Ward felt embarrassed and replied, "I'm sorry to be so obvious, but I just feel I owe it to Jerry to do something other than sit back and let the State Police do the only investigating or questioning. We all did that once and nothing came of it. Do you remember what any of the others did that day?"

"You don't have to apologize to me," Carmen answered. "If anybody owes Uncle Jerry anything, it's me. I'm not at all positive what everyone did. All the kids—Jim's three, Bill's one, and Maria's two—were up early to catch the milk truck up the valley where they hiked to the fire tower. Jim's wife and Bill's went to Albany shopping and didn't get back until nearly dark. They took my father as far as Catskill and left him there—to visit some of his old cronies, so he said—most likely to get drunk. Someone—I don't know who it was—brought him home just before I got there. Jim, Bill, and Maria all went off separately. Each went on one of those motor scooters, but I don't know where they went or what they did. I might have known then, but if I did, I've forgotten now."

The next was a tough question, but Ward had to ask it. "Do you have any idea who might have killed Jerry or why?"

"I just don't think it was any of us, no matter how much the police may think so. None of us had any reason to; if anything, we all had reason to help him if we had known he needed help. He and my father argued a lot; my father mostly, but I don't think even he would do anything like that."

That seemed to end the questioning. At least Ward couldn't think of any more sensible questions so he changed the subject to ask Carmen about some of the climbs she had recently made. She brightened then and told him a long tale about an expedition the year before with an all-women's climb on Mt. McKinley (only she called it Denali) in Alaska. She had been one of three summiters and was proud of her accomplishment. She said she hoped Uncle Jerry had been looking down at her as she topped the final, rounded snow slope to stand on the top of the mountain.

By the time Ward and Carmen walked back across the field to the farmhouse, most of the guests and friends had left. He saw Jim motioning and, when he reached the house, Jim asked if he could spare a few minutes more to talk over the plans the family now had for the farm.

Jim had always been the one "in charge." That was only natural — he was the oldest of the four children and during their early years someone had to bring some organization and direction into their lives and Jim stepped into the breech left by their father's absences after their mother had died. No one around the valley knew just what had happened to the so-called "gypsy woman" who was their mother. The speculations ran rampant fueled by the early stories told by Sarah, Larry and Jerry's mother, soon after Larry had run off with her or, as Sarah said, "when she seduced him." It hadn't all been a scandal, so Ward had learned from Jim after he came to work on the survey crew. His mother had died following a long illness, Jim said. His father had cared for her as best he could and for the children too, for that matter, but nothing helped and she had just faded away. They were living in Texas then and Jim said his father worked at jobs 'round and about, but after his mother died he seemed to lose interest in everything and took to staying away more and more. Jim had tried to hold things together, tried to see they had something to eat, went to school on time, and kept up with their studies. Finally, their father settled down enough to realize he had to do something about the children, had to find some sort of a home for them. That's when he packed them up, sold what few belongings they had, and brought them to South Branch, the farm, and Uncle Jerry.

It was a couple of years after that when Jerry came to Ward with the idea of putting Jim to work on the survey crew for the summer. "I can't have all four of those damn kids around under foot all summer," Jerry had said. "Besides, I want 'em to find out there's something else in this world other than milkin' cows, cuttin' hay, and shovelin' manure. And, I want somebody other than me tellin' 'em what to do once in a while. I don't think they listen to me half the time and it'll do 'em good to find out when somebody else says something, they mean business." Ward knew it was all bluster and noticed how the subject of Jim coming to work on the crew had expanded right in the middle of Jerry's tirade to "them" or " 'em." Ward could see what Jerry had in mind; each summer, one or more of Larry's kids was to be parceled out to the survey crew until the last one got out of high school.

Ward didn't much care for the idea of acting as baby sitter for the summer and said so. But Jerry was persuasive. "If Jim don't work the way you want him to, let me know and I'll see that he does and when he don't give you a day's work, I'll pay you his wages for that day." It had never come to that; all four of the Ford children had given a hard day of work for every day of pay. Of course, things weren't always smooth, some upsets happened now and then — Carmen quit every once in awhile and Maria sometimes spent more time daydreaming than working, but all in all, Ward never regretted taking on "those damn kids." He always suspected they received at least one lecture a week about being a responsible person, doing what they were told, listening when somebody told them how and why to do something, not complaining even when they had something to complain about, and solving their own problems. At least, every time Ward started a lecture on one of those subjects, the Ford kid being lectured would say "We've already heard that one."

As the younger Ford children came on the crew, they complained about how bossy Jim was. Ward suspected that was true and probably necessary as far as his brother and sisters were concerned, but he never had found him that way. Jim seemed to know he was on the crew for the experience of learning about work, life, and the things that made them important.

Now, however, Jim was in charge and asked Ward to come with him into the workshop. Ward had been there before and marveled at the order of it; everything was always in its place. It was not full of clutter and confusion like most farm workshops. It was Jerry's workshop, of course, his methodical ways were obvious in every corner of it. He had built it himself as an extension on the end of the barn. It was here that Jerry kept all his tools and repaired whatever needed repairing and built whatever needed building so that the farm kept running as efficiently as it should. On entering, Ward looked in the far corner at the empty hook and remembered, as Carmen had said, the rucksack that always before had hung there.

The door to the small safe under the main workbench stood open; it was empty, but a strong box that had probably been in it was on the bench. "I guess none of us ever knew how Uncle Jerry made his money. He helped us all, you know, in one way or another. I wouldn't be nearly as well off as I am if he hadn't paid my way through school. Now I have my own insurance office in New Jersey, not a very big one, of course, but mine just the same. I didn't really know what I wanted to do when I finished high school. I liked the survey work I did with you, but I knew I wouldn't be good enough at it to make it a career. Uncle Jerry said he thought I had a head for business and why didn't I go to a good business school and maybe while I was there, I would make up my mind. We sent for a lot of school catalogs and, between us, we picked out what we thought was a good one and I've never regretted the decision. Once I tried to thank him for what he did, but he said that was all over and done with and just forget it.

"When we opened the safe and this strong box, we found out where Uncle Jerry got his money. The farm certainly didn't pay enough to do all the extra things he did for each of us. He was a banker. He loaned money out at a rate of interest a point or two above bank interest, but that was fair because he didn't require any security other than a signed note and didn't hound people if they were late with a payment now and then. All these papers are those notes, must be well over two hundred of them dating back to the 1920s. Each one is paid in full with a record of every payment carefully set down on the back of each note. Some of them are for people two and three counties away.

"But that's not what I wanted to talk about. We found Uncle Jerry's will in here and my father's will also. Maria called the nursing home in Yuba City, California, and talked with him. He's not very well, but his mind is sharp. He says this is the only will he ever made and he doesn't want to change it. As you know, we all came here now because seven years have passed since Uncle Jerry disappeared. That's the statute of limitations, or so we thought, here in New York State, and we wanted to see if we could have him declared legally dead and go about dividing his estate however the law requires us to while our father is still alive. We never quite got started when you found the body. . .or the skeleton, I should say. Now we're back to square one.

"The wills are both the same. My father says that when he got here back in 1955, Uncle Jerry already had both wills drawn up and suggested they go to the lawyer to get them signed and so they did. Now that we have confirmation of Uncle Jerry's death, the lawyer says we can process the will and distribute the estate the way it provides. The only specific provision in the will is that Bill is to get all the books in the library. Everything else is to be sold, including the farm, with the proceeds to be put in a trust fund in favor of the surviving brother, which is, of course, now my father. Money can be drawn from the trust to pay for normal living costs, medical expenses, and so forth for him. On his death, the funds of the trust are to be split equally among us four children or, if any one of us predeceases him, that one-quarter share is to be split equally among his or her surviving children. It's a typical Uncle Jerry document, all thought out and everything covered.

"We've talked among ourselves and none of us wants to buy the farm or any part of it. All of us are settled someplace else now—except for Carmen, who will probably never settle anywhere—and don't want to come back, especially now we know Uncle Jerry was murdered here. We've also talked to Russ Schermerhorn next door. He's offered a fair price and we've decided to take it. That's where you come in; we have to have the farm surveyed. Only now, instead of dividing it into two shares and then somehow splitting those, we just want the outbounds run with a description written for a deed to Russ and another description to convey the right in the spring to the State."

Ward agreed to the change in the survey and said he would get it done as soon as he could. It would now be easier than before, so he could complete it in a month or so, he thought. That business out of the way, he turned the conversation to Jerry's murder and his interest in asking the family members some questions about it and otherwise doing some snooping around on his own. Jim replied that he had no objection to that and was sure the others wouldn't either. He didn't think the State Police were making much headway in their investigation and thought maybe someone else asking some questions would be of help. But, Jim advised, he had better start soon because he and his family were leaving tomorrow and Carmen was leaving tonight. Bill and Maria were staying on for a few more days; Bill to start packing the books and Maria to go through the house to retrieve anything of their father's to take back to him.

Jim anticipated the first question. "I suppose, like the State Police, you wonder where I was the day of the murder—now that we know it was a murder. Bryan and his people have pretty much run that one around with all of us. Of course, seven years does something to your memory, you understand." Ward acknowledged that he did, pointing out to Jim that he had a few years on him and as he got older he'd find out that memory got worse instead of better.

Jim continued, "I went fishing, down the Schoharie below Lexington in the morning and, then, up the Batavia Kill in the afternoon. Somewhere Bill got hold of a number of those motor scooters that were popular back then. Rented them, I think, and brought them here on that little trailer he built to haul stuff behind his car. I took one of those and left it along the stream while I fished a while and then walked back to it and moved it along to the next fishing spot now and then. It worked out a lot better than a car; much easier to park along the road. I saw a number of other fishermen during the day, but didn't recognize them and didn't talk to any of them. Most fishermen don't want to do much else but fish you know, they don't want to stand around and talk."

"Do you remember what any of the others did?" Ward asked.

"Jenny, my wife, and Bill's wife went to Albany shopping. I remember that so well because Jenny came back with bag after bag of new clothes—bargains she said—but wouldn't tell me how much money she spent and we got into a little tiff over that. They took my father along as far as Catskill, where they dropped him off. I don't remember how he got home—some friend brought him, I guess. The kids were all up and gone early; they caught the milk truck on its way up the valley and then hiked up to the fire tower.

I really don't recall what the others did, but knowing Carmen, I expect she went off climbing somewhere."

"Can you think of any reason why anyone would want to kill your Uncle Jerry?"

Jim replied with a slow shake of his head from side to side. "That's the craziest part of it all. If it had been my father, nobody would have thought twice about why. He irritated a lot of people in his time and I'm sure some were mad enough now and then to do him in — they were twins; maybe someone took Uncle Jerry for my father. I never thought of that before. Anyway, no one would ever have gotten that mad at Uncle Jerry. He never did anything to hurt anyone. Oh, lots of people thought he was odd — he wasn't, but he encouraged everyone to think so just so they wouldn't bother him — but that's no reason to kill anyone."

"Speaking of odd," Ward said, "Do you remember anything odd happening that day? Anything that didn't fit with the usual routine?"

"Yes, the hammer. It was gone, but I didn't notice that until a few days later when I needed it for some work I was doing — repairing the railing on the front steps, I think. You can see how orderly Uncle Jerry has things in here. Every tool has its own place where it's to be hung. He even painted an outline of each one on the wall so it would always be put back in the same place. Well, when I needed a hammer, I came here to get it, but the space for it was empty and I couldn't find it anyplace else either. The one hanging there now is one I bought up in Hunter to replace it."

While Ward had some more questions he wanted to ask Jim, their conversation was cut short when Jenny came in the workshop and said they had to pack that afternoon if they were going to leave early the next morning. However, Ward thought it probably didn't make much difference anyway; all he was finding out so far were things that only deepened the mystery. Now he was reasonably sure he had found the murder weapon; well, found wasn't the right word. More correctly, he felt he knew where the murder weapon had come from — he had made up his mind it had been a hammer when he first saw the circular impressions in Jerry's skull — but he sure didn't know where it was now. Neither did anyone else, except, of course, the murderer and he didn't know who that was either.

The next morning Ward returned to the farmhouse and found Maria in the kitchen as he knew he would. She and Carmen were exact opposites — Carmen was the rugged, outdoorsey type and Maria was the ideal housewife, if such a designation existed. While Carmen shunned domesticity, Maria sought it.

The first summer Maria came on the survey crew, Ward was sure that Jerry's experiment would fail right there. Jim and Bill had been assets to the crew and he was sure Carmen would be also when her turn came a couple of years later. But Maria was a different story. Not only were women a novelty on a survey crew in those days (and still were), Maria was not the one to break new ground, not the one to be the first to move into what had heretofore been a domain exclusive to men. However, Ward needn't have worried — Jerry had prepared Maria with one of his usual lectures. She had been told not to complain about what she was asked to do, just do it; not to find fault with working conditions, she was going to get sweaty and dirty, it was part of the job; she was going to get paid for a day's work, so she was to make sure that's what she earned; and so on. Maria was outfitted the way she was supposed to be — Jerry had gotten hold of an L. L. Bean catalog and he and Maria had picked out everything she would need for a job in the woods.

It wasn't easy for her, but she had listened when she should have and after a month or so she developed into a productive member of the survey crew. She didn't become particularly adept at swinging an ax, but made every effort to improve at it. And she never did quite get the knack of "throwing" the chain. The 66-foot steel chain is divided into 100 links. In order to do it up into a single loop, the chainman holds the 0 mark upright in his (or her, in Maria's case) left hand and lays the 8-link mark, then the 16-link mark, then the 24-link mark, and so on, over it until the entire chain hangs in a figure-eight. The chainman then holds the lower strands of the chain at the cross in the figure-eight in his left hand, the upper strands in his right hand and pulls his hands in opposite directions while giving a deft twist to his right hand and the strands of the chain held by it. If done properly, the chain will snap into a single loop, four links in circumference. If not done properly, the tape can fall into a mess of tangled coils and the chain has to be threaded carefully out of the entanglement, laid flat on the ground, and the whole process started over. Maria always seemed to go through at least one such entanglement every time she did up the chain, but usually made it on the second try. When she finally had the chain in a loop, she wrapped the long, leather thongs that hung on the metal rings at each end of the tape around and around the layers of the chain and tied the ends of them into a neat bow to add a feminine touch to a once manly process.

Maria spent three summers on the survey crew. If she had a fault, it was that she was forever falling in love. No one wanted the proverbial cottage for two or three or more as much as she did. No one wanted to be swept off her feet by a prince charming more than Maria did and she was always on the lookout for him. She met him — or so she thought — after high school, when she was going to a small secretarial school in Albany. Jerry absolutely forbid their marriage until she completed school and wasn't too happy about it even then — he had misgivings about the man's reliability and ambition from the first time he met him. He relented in the end — Larry didn't have an opinion one way or another — after Maria assured him that her intended was really the prince charming she had always searched for. He wasn't, as it turned out.

Maria's husband was one of those people who is never happy for long with what he is doing or where he is. After a few months of living in one place and working (when he would) at one job after another, he wanted to go someplace different, where the weather was warmer, where the pay was higher, where the rent was cheaper, and so on and so on. So they moved from place to place around the country—the twin boys were born in Kentucky where their father worked for a short time on a horse farm. They ended up in California and when he wanted to move on from there, he didn't tell Maria about it. He just went and left her and the boys behind to fend for themselves as best they could. She never knew where he went and never heard from him again. Neither did she ever fall in love again—if a prince charming was really out there somewhere, he'd have to find her because she gave up her search for him.

She invited Ward to sit down at the kitchen (in Jerry's side of the house) table and poured him a cup of coffee. She asked if he wanted some bacon and eggs or anything, but he declined, saying he had eaten his breakfast at home and really couldn't eat another one. The sink was full of dishes and Maria went happily about the task of washing and drying them. Jim and his family and Bill's wife and daughter had driven away only a few minutes before Ward arrived, she said and she had made all of them eat a good breakfast before they left. Bill was in the library at the front of the house and she knew he would want to see Ward while he was here.

She seemed to want to talk while she was at the sink and Ward thought it best to let her rather than interrupting with what he had come to believe were a lot of inane questions. He lit up his pipe and leaned back in his chair, the cup of coffee near at hand.

"Uncle Jerry was a good man. I don't know how any of us would have turned out if he hadn't been around to keep us on the straight and narrow. My father has never been given the credit he should either. He knew, after our mother died, that he wouldn't make much of a home for us, so he brought us here where we would be under Uncle Jerry's influence and watchful eye. He knew Uncle Jerry would rant and rave and threaten to throw us all out, but he also knew where his heart was and that he'd take us under his wing and make something out of us or know the reason why. We all let Uncle Jerry down lots of times, but he always forgave us after we had listened to the usual lecture. We heard some of those so many times we could repeat them word for word.

"You must know how reluctant I was to go to work for you that first summer. I really didn't want to; I couldn't think of anything worse than clomping around the woods all day, getting dirty, and running into snakes and things. It didn't make any difference—Uncle Jerry said I was going and that was that. I did enjoy the work, once I found out what was going on and why each part of the survey was being done. I wouldn't want to do it again though, but I'm glad to have had the experience.

"I wanted to be a housewife and a mother. I thought, at first, that my dreams had come true, but it turned out to be a nightmare. Uncle Jerry insisted I had to learn a trade or a skill or something so that I could take care of myself if my dream marriage fell apart. 'All marriages aren't made in Heaven, you know,' he said to me more than once. I didn't want to wait until I went through school and learned all about office work and management, but, again, Uncle Jerry prevailed and I did what he wanted. Now, I'm glad I did. He paid all the costs of that school — it isn't any wonder the farm began to deteriorate back then. He spent all the money that should have gone into the upkeep of it on us kids, sending us to school and whatnot.

"When my husband left us out in California, the twins were little and I had to take care of them as well as myself. Actually, it was easier after he left, at least I didn't have to support him during the times he didn't have work or wouldn't work. I got a job as a secretary at a small business then; now I'm the manager of that same office although it's a lot bigger now. Still, it wasn't all a piece of cake and Uncle Jerry knew that. From the time my husband left, Uncle Jerry sent me a check every month up until the time he too disappeared, or was murdered, I guess I should say. It wasn't much, but it sure helped. I didn't ask for it, he just sent it. He disappeared just about the time the twins were ready to start college and medical school. Fortunately, they got some grants and loans so that they could go. Now they're nearly finished. I think some of Uncle Jerry's perserverance descended down to them — he would be proud of them."

The dishes were washed and dried by then. Maria poured herself a cup of coffee and sat down across the kitchen table from Ward. "Do you remember anything unusual about the day Jerry disappeared?" he asked.

"When the State Police people asked me that, do you know, I couldn't even remember what I did that day. It seemed such a jumble-up time that couple of weeks. All of us were here and people were coming and going all the time and it's difficult to sort out one day from another. So I guess that day wasn't much more unusual than any other."

"Did you go anywhere that day?" Ward next asked.

"Like I told the troopers, the only way I can remember what I did is by remembering what everyone else did. The funny thing was that Uncle Jerry was gone and so was his truck. We all talked about it at breakfast because he always ate with us when he came in from the barn and that morning he didn't come in. Then someone realized the truck was gone and the animals hadn't been taken care of. That all seemed odd, but we knew Uncle Jerry always had a logical reason for everything he did and would explain it to us when he got back. But he didn't come back.

"Then I remembered that the kids were gone too that morning. They had gotten up before anyone and were off on an all-day hike to the fire tower on Hunter Mountain. Bill and Jim's wives went to Albany right after breakfast—they took my father along as far as Catskill. After Carmen, Bill, and Jim finished the morning farm chores, they all left on their own. I don't know where they went, but they each took one of those motor scooters Bill had rented someplace in Pennsylvania and brought with him.

"I realized then that I was the only one still at the farm. After I finished the breakfast dishes and cleaned up around, I made up my mind I would go someplace too, so I packed a lunch and went on a ride around the mountains on the last of the motor scooters."

"Where did you go?"

"I didn't really 'go' anywhere," Maria answered. "Since the whole trip was kind of a spur-of-the-moment thing, I didn't have any route planned out. Mostly, I rode around the northern end of the Catskills—East Windham, Cornwallville, Durham, Gilboa, and places like that. I remember I ate my lunch where the road goes around Mt. Pisgah above Durham—I sat there on a rock and watched the view out over the Hudson River and on up toward Albany while I ate."

"Did you see anyone you knew or stop along the way to visit some old friend?"

"No. I didn't stop anywhere. I didn't even have to stop for gas—the motor scooter was full when I started and those things go forever on a tank of gas. I didn't see anyone I knew, but I saw a lot of people out on their lawns and working in their gardens when I drove by, so they must have seen me."

"What time did you get back to the farm?" Ward asked.

"I don't remember that. Some were home by then and others weren't, but I don't remember who was and who wasn't. It really wasn't a day that would stand out in anyone's memory. It was just a pleasant day and that's how I recall it. Of course, if we had known then what was to follow, we would have had more reason to remember. It was only after Uncle Jerry didn't return by the next day that anybody got worried."

"Do you have any ideas about what must have happened? Why Jerry was at the big rock? How the truck got to the railroad station at Hudson?" Ward realized these were the puzzling questions he had been asking himself all along.

"I guess that's what all of us want to know," Maria replied. "We've pretty well decided that we're never going to know the answers."

Ward had just about concluded he wasn't going to get any of those answers either. He guessed he'd better stick to surveying. However, he had gone this far, he might just as well keep on. He thanked Maria for the coffee and she thanked him for being a good listener. She had needed someone to talk to about Uncle Jerry, she said, and Ward had happened along at just the right time. She told him to go down the hall toward the front of the house and he would find Bill in the library on the left side of the hall just before he got to the front door.

If Ward had a favorite of the Ford children, it was Bill. The other three had come to work for their summers because they were sent. Bill had come with an eager anticipation. He wasn't so much interested in land surveying itself as he was in the mathematics of it. In those days all surveying computations were done longhand by using logarithms and traverse tables. Calculators hadn't quite yet taken the place of "a head for figures," which Bill certainly had. Ward also enjoyed the intricacies of the computations and he and Bill were forever in a contest to see who could first complete figuring a long traverse or determine the acreage of a multi-sided parcel of land. Each especially relished catching the other in a simple error in addition or subtraction. They each concocted complex mathematical problems and challenged the other to solve them. When one couldn't, the other beamed as if he had won a major prize.

Ward wasn't surprised when Bill announced at the beginning of his last summer on the survey crew that he was going to college and when he got done he was going to be a mathematics teacher. And that's just what he became. He married a delightful girl he met in college and, when his resume' was accepted at a high school in Pennsylvania, she submitted hers also and became an English teacher at the same school. They were both still there — the only break had been when she took some time off when their daughter and only child was born. They were completely happy in what they did and in each other.

Bill's other passion was books and Ward thought it only right when Jim had told him that Jerry's will provided the library was to go to Bill. The library was a curious thing — Ward had never been in it because Jerry wouldn't allow him or anyone else except Bill in the room. It was a big room at the front of the farmhouse — on Jerry's side of the building. The room itself had probably been a parlor at the time Caleb Ford built the house. It was Josiah Ford who turned it into a library when he came back to the farm to live with his wife and twin sons in 1900. The curious part was that it was always locked. The single door leading into the room off the hall was solid oak with a substantial lock built into it. As if that wasn't enough, the two windows on the front and the one on the side of the house were all fitted with iron bars much like those on the windows of a jail cell. Jerry had once told Ward his father had fortified the room because so many of his books were valuable first editions and he didn't want any burglars to be able to get at them. However, times change — as Ward went down the hall, he saw the door to the library was opened wide and he could hear Bill inside, packing the books, he supposed.

Bill noticed Ward standing in the doorway and greeted him. "Hi! Come on in; Jim said you'd be stopping by to visit."

Ward paused before entering; he was just amazed by the furnishings of the room or, better put, by the few of them. Right in the middle of the room was an old flat-topped desk with a wooden swivel chair drawn up under it. In front of the desk was a big, upholstered chair with a small stand beside it and a gooseneck lamp set so that it provided light for both the chair and the desk. And that was it, except for the bookshelves. All the walls, from floor to ceiling, were lined with bookshelves built against them — the only spaces not covered by shelves were the three windows, the doorway, and the big iron radiator set across the room against the outside wall. And each shelf was filled with books except the few that Bill had emptied. The books from these were packed in cardboard boxes and other empty boxes were scattered about the wide-open floor. Bill had a long job ahead of him.

"Have you ever seen so many books in one room except at a library?" Bill asked.

Ward could only shake his head in disbelief. He knew the room was a library because Jerry Ford had told him so, but he hadn't realized what a large library it was. It was certainly unique for South Branch, he thought, and, probably, for the whole of Greene County.

Bill continued, "Sit down in the easy chair so we can talk more comfortably."

As Ward settled in the big chair, Bill pulled out the swivel chair and sat in it, looking quizzically across the desk at Ward. "Jim said you wanted to ask me some questions. I don't know what I can tell you that you haven't heard already from the others, but go ahead and ask."

"I don't know what you can tell me either," Ward began, "but I just feel I have to find out as much as I can about the day Jerry disappeared. Can you remember what you did that day?"

"I can now, but I probably wouldn't have a week or so ago. When the State Police asked me the same question, my memory was a complete blank. But the longer I thought about it, the more things came back to me. You don't suppose they suspect one of us murdered Uncle Jerry, do you? The questions they asked would make you think so. I don't know how they could think that. Of course, they don't know how much Uncle Jerry did for each of us. If they did, they would go looking someplace else."

Ward agreed with Bill, but pointed out, "They have to do their job and part of that is asking a lot of questions that don't seem to make any sense at the time."

"Yeah, I suppose so," Bill responded. "Well, anyway, it wasn't the most memorable day. At least it wasn't then. If we had known what had happened, what the rest of us did would have stuck in our minds. I'm sure someone already told you about the kids and their day at the fire tower. And about how Jim's wife and mine went to Albany and took my father with them as far as Catskill. I went off by myself on one of those motor scooters I brought with me when I came in June, right after school was out. A friend of mine, who runs a garage down the street from where we live, had a whole bunch of them for rent. He talked me into renting some to take along for our summer in the country. So I did. I loaded them on that little flat-bed trailer I built and dragged them all the way here. I don't think my wife was very happy about it, but she never makes a fuss. Anyway, I drove over to the Peekamoose and went hiking up Stone Cabin Brook; over Van Wyck Mountain to the top of Table, Lone, Rocky, and Peekamoose mountains; and then down Bear Hole Brook back to the road. It was a long day and a long hike—I had done it before when I was a kid and enjoyed it so much then, I had to see if I could do it again. A couple of times along the way I wasn't so sure it had been such a good idea."

There goes another motor scooter traveling around all by itself, Ward thought; a good thing Bill brought them along, or everyone would have had to stay at the farmhouse. "Did you see anyone on your way back and forth or on the hike?"

"No, those were all trailless peaks back then—I don't know if they are yet—and I didn't see a soul all day except, of course, those I saw on the roads I drove along."

"Didn't any of you wonder when you realized that Jerry had left in the morning without doing the chores, especially leaving the cows unmilked?"

"Oh, I suppose we did," Bill answered. "But Uncle Jerry sometimes did unpredictable things. Not often, mind you, but once in a while he would depart from his usual methodical ways and the strict routine he followed. He also could be quite secretive about what he was thinking and what he knew. For instance, he helped all of us by paying for college, but he did it quietly and told each of us not to tell the others about it. Of course, we knew—we were a pretty close bunch and we each knew that, while we had been awarded some scholarships, they weren't enough to pay all the costs. And we certainly didn't get any help from our father."

"Speaking of your father, do you think he could have killed his twin brother?"

"No," Bill replied. "If he had been the one killed, I could believe that Uncle Jerry might have done it. He sure could exasperate Uncle Jerry. But my father realized Uncle Jerry had been the answer to four motherless kids and, for all his other faults, wouldn't have done anything to upset that along the way. However, by that time, we were all grown up and my father does have a mean streak when he drinks too much."

"Had Jerry been acting strangely before that day?"

The answer was totally unexpected. "Yes," Bill said, "he'd been acting strange for two or three years before that. Maybe it's good we're here in the library because that's part of the strangeness. It's a long story, but for starters, I know what the key is for that you found along with the other stuff in Uncle Jerry's pocket. It's the key to the family treasure. Or, at least, that's what he thought it was to."

Ward sat bolt upright in his chair. "The family treasure! What family treasure?"

"That's what the long story is. All of us knew about the family treasure because our father used to talk about it once in awhile. But he said it was all in his mother's mind, so we never paid much attention to it whenever he or Uncle Jerry mentioned it. I asked Uncle Jerry once what he thought and he said the same as my father had said. He didn't think his mother was crazy or anything like that, but he said his father was always telling her things that weren't true and she believed him anyway. He thought it was just another of my grandfather's stories. But then, a few years before he disappeared, he found the key and that changed his whole thinking about the treasure. In fact, he became obsessed with it and that's when he started acting strange.

"This library was my grandfather's. Uncle Jerry told me that he—his name was Josiah—had worked for some well-to-do family over in the Hardenburgh country. In fact, that's where my grandmother came from and where my father and Uncle Jerry were born. It seems the family liked Josiah very much and, when they realized how much he liked books—must be that's where I got it from—began giving him great numbers of them that they picked up on their travels abroad. When my grandfather and grandmother came back to this farm around 1900, they brought all the books with them. Josiah took over this room and built these bookshelves. Uncle Jerry said they weren't all full then, but my grandfather kept buying books and, when he died, the library was just as you see it now. The winter before he died, Uncle Jerry told me, his father put those bars on the windows and replaced the door with that thick oak one that's there now.

"My grandmother got quite disgusted with my grandfather for throwing away so much money on books. Uncle Jerry said they used to argue about it a lot and my grandfather would always say to her, 'All we have to do is be patient; someday our ship will come in and we'll be able to spend the treasure that's on it.' Uncle Jerry said he heard his father say that or that they would find it at the end of the rainbow at least a hundred times. After Josiah drowned in the flood and things really got tough, my grandmother used to tell Uncle Jerry to be patient, someday, when the treasure could be spent, they would have all the money they needed.

"Uncle Jerry got the library from my grandfather. I don't know if it was in a will or not, but somehow he and my father both understood that, while they were to have an equal share of everything else that made up the property, the library was Uncle Jerry's. He kept it locked, except for the times he was in it, mostly to protect the books that were there, he said. Uncle

Jerry wasn't much of a reader, but when he realized what a bookworm I was, he used to let me in the library with the understanding that I couldn't take anything out of the room. I had many happy hours in here; I read a lot of the books, but nowhere near all of them. Uncle Jerry and I spent a lot of time together in this room when I was growing up and in the years later when I came back to visit him for a couple of weeks each summer. It was during those times when he told me about my grandfather and grandmother and the treasure.

"As I said, Uncle Jerry didn't put much stock in the treasure story. However, one summer — must have been about four summers before he disappeared — the minute I got here, he took me into the library and locked the door behind us even though no one else was around. He said that a few weeks earlier he had noticed the second shelf up on the tier of shelves over there in the corner had a crack in it and was sagging. He had taken all the books off that shelf and off the one next to the floor below it and had taken the cracked shelf out so he could measure it and build a new one to replace it. When he removed the shelf, he found a nail driven into the side wall, way in the back, and up under where the cracked shelf had been. Hanging on the nail was an old key. He had left the nail there and the key hanging on it. The only way we could see it was to lay down on the floor and look up into the corner. With the shelves and books in place, the key was absolutely hidden. His father must have put it there, Uncle Jerry thought because no one else was allowed in the library while he was alive and since he had died no one but the two of us had been in the room. It must be the key to the treasure after all, Uncle Jerry said. He had tried the key in every lock and padlock he could find all over the farm, but it didn't fit any of them.

"That's when Uncle Jerry began to act strange. He thought that because the key was in the library, something else in the library must tell where the lock was that it fit. He had taken every book off every shelf and looked for hidden panels, but hadn't found any. He was then convinced the answer must be in one of the books, and that was why his father had barred the windows and otherwise been so possessive of them. He decided he would go through every book, page by page, and look for some markings or, perhaps, pin pricks under the letters or words on some page that spelled out a message. And that's just what he did from then until he disappeared. Every free waking moment he had, he was in the library going over page after page, book after book. That's why he wouldn't go to the movies with us the night before he disappeared; he was in the library, still on the search."

Ward had been positively fascinated by the whole story. As Bill concluded the narrative, Ward was silent too, not knowing what to say or what question to ask. Finally, he snapped to. "Do you think Jerry found what he was looking for?"

"No, not really. Because I don't think anything was out there or in the books to be found. I'll bet more than once you've said to Betty, 'Someday our ship will come in.' I know I've said it. That's a standard statement used in every family—except those where everyone is born with a silver spoon in their mouth. Their ship has already come in and they don't have to wait for it. I didn't know my grandfather and grandmother. They were both dead when my father brought us here. But from what I've heard him and Uncle Jerry tell about them, that would be a typical thing for him to say to her to quiet down her finding fault and that she would believe completely. I think Uncle Jerry just realized he was on the downhill side of life and was grasping at every straw he could to make his fortune—most likely to leave to us."

Ward, however, was not convinced. "What did the State Police think when you told them about the key?"

"I didn't tell them. For all I know, Uncle Jerry could have carried that key around from the first day he told me about it. After that day, I never looked for it under the bookshelf until the troopers told us about finding it on the big rock. It wasn't hanging on the nail then, but it might not have been there for the years in between. If my grandfather first put it there, it would had to have been before 1905 or 1906, whenever he died, so it could have been there for nearly fifty years. A lot of locks would have come and gone on the farm in that time. Just because Uncle Jerry couldn't find one the key fit doesn't mean anything."

"Well, I suppose," Ward responded, "but it does seem more than coincidence that he had the key with him. How do you explain the fact of the truck being found all the way over in Hudson?"

Bill chuckled at that. "This isn't like one of those mathematical puzzles we used to throw at one another. I'm afraid we're not going to come up with a finite answer to this like we were able to do with those."

Ward finally had to agree. It seemed as if he had been running this puzzle around in his head for years. He got up from his chair and walked over to the line of bookshelves against one of the walls. "Do you know how your Uncle Jerry was making his search through the books? Was he reading each one or was he just scanning each page?"

"I don't think he was reading them. He very carefully looked at every page though, including the covers, inside and out. He didn't know exactly what to look for. I was in here with him a few times and watched him now and then when I happened to glance up from the book I was reading. He examined each page for some mark, such as an underline of a word or a letter. Then he'd hold the page up to the light to see if any pin pricks were through the page under various of the letters. He even turned each page sideways and upside down. He did that book by book, shelf by shelf, and was working his way around the room. He started over by the door at the top shelf, looked at each book in order across that shelf and then did the same thing for the next shelf down and so on. He was always sure to keep the books in the same order as they came off the shelf. He thought maybe only one word would be marked in a book and that the next word in the message would be in a following book somewhere further along that shelf or on the next one down."

"Do you know where he was along the shelves? Do you know what shelf or what book he had worked up to that night you all went to the movies?"

"No, and the reason I don't know is because, as time went on, he became more secretive. That first summer he let me be in the library with him. When I came to visit the next summer, he would let me in the library to pick out a book, but I had to take it out of the room to read if he was going to be in here on his search. He wouldn't even talk about it after that, but I knew what was going on just by the way he acted."

"Did Jim or your sisters or your father know about the key or about Jerry's belief that some message might be in the books?"

"As I said, we all knew about the so-called family treasure, but I'm positive that Uncle Jerry and I were the only ones who knew about the key and the book business."

By this time Ward had looked at many of the books. It certainly was some collection. He wasn't much of an authority, but he was sure that most of the books were first editions. He noticed that a lot of them had been rebound in leather with the color or shade or texture of the leather being different for different authors. Bill noticed that Ward was looking at one set of the leather-bound books. "I don't know if that rebinding was a good idea or not," Bill said. "When that was done, the original covers were destroyed and that's part of the value of a first edition. On the other hand, a specially bound set of first editions is worth something extra, too. It's six of one and half-a-dozen of the other, I guess."

"I would think the bound volumes would have a longer lifespan too," Ward said. "However, I'm no expert, the only books I have that even resemble a collection are those by Arthur Conan Doyle. I think I have every one of his books now, but I don't think any of them are first editions. I put that set together just because his writing is so good. Like everyone else, I like the Sherlock Holmes stories, but I enjoy those with Professor Challenger and the ones about Brigadier Gerard just as much."

While Ward was talking, Bill went over to one of the lower shelves next to the single window on the far wall and took down a set of five books, each bound in a dark-brown leather cover with the title and author of each in gold lettering on the front cover and spine.

"Here," said Bill as he handed the five books to Ward. "I've always wanted to give you something as thanks for those summers I worked with you, but never could think of anything suitable. These books are just the thing."

Ward thought to decline Bill's generosity, but realized that might offend him, so he accepted the gift. All five books were by Conan Doyle and were the first of the nine in the Sherlock Holmes series.

"These should fit well in your collection," Bill said. "They are all first English editions. They're the Sherlock Holmes books that were published up to my grandfather's death; the rest were published after that although I think one was published that same year, but it doesn't seem to have been added to his library. At least I can't find it here."

Ward was genuinely pleased with the gift of the books and said so. "These really are treasures. Maybe you're right that the family treasure is this library."

By then the morning was over and Ward didn't want to hold Bill up from his packing any longer. He'd run out of questions anyway and was, in fact, beginning to think that any questioning or investigating might better be left to the police after all. He thanked Bill again for the books, said he'd stop in before he left for Pennsylvania and walked down the hall back toward the kitchen. Maria was no longer there, so he went on out the back door where he found her weeding the flower bed. He talked a little about the weather, how well the weeds grew when it was hot and dry as it always was in these July days, and said he would visit her again before she left for California and home.

The rest of the day passed quickly for Ward. He had some deed work to do in the County Clerk's Office in Catskill and that took his mind off the morning, the questions, and everything else to do with Jerry Ford and the fate that had befallen him. After supper, he lit up his pipe as usual and settled down in his easy chair in the front room. Betty was off to a meeting of her sewing circle and he was going to spend the evening looking through the five books Bill had given him.

He tried to put them in order by date as best he could, trying to remember when they were published before he opened any of them. The first was *A Study in Scarlet* published in 1888 by Ward, Lock and Co., London; New York. They were the first English editions all right or, at least, this one was, he thought to himself as he ran his fingers over the soft leather binding. The second was *The Sign of Four* published in 1890 by Spencer Blackett, London. The third was *The Adventures of Sherlock Holmes* published in 1892 by George Newnes, Ltd., London. He had them right so far, Ward smiled to himself. The fourth was *The Memoirs of Sherlock Holmes* published in 1894 by George Newnes, Ltd., London; and the last was *The Hound of the Baskervilles* published in 1902 also by George Newnes, Ltd., London.

Ward sat contented with the five books on his lap. He had, of course, read the stories in them many times before. He had some favorites like most other people, but he thought reading them again in a first edition would be an experience to savor. He picked up one at random — it turned out to be *The Memoirs* — to look more closely at the binding. He opened the front cover expecting to see Josiah Ford's bookplate, but it was clean and, therefore, not blemished by some stuck-in reference to the owner. The inside of the back cover did, however, have some writing on it. Across the top of the blank page facing the cover was written the inscription "1 step or pace = 1 chain."

Ward had never run across a scale like that in all his years of surveying and map making. "1 step or pace = 1 chain," he repeated out loud. "That's certainly a curious annotat. . . ."

That's as far as Ward Eastman got with that thought because another one crowded it out of his mind. He jumped out of his chair, the other four books tumbling onto the floor; hastily dropped his pipe into the ash tray (and missed it); and ran out of the room clutching *The Memoirs of Sherlock Holmes* to his chest.

The Windham Journal
Windham, New York
Thursday, August 16, 1962

Obituaries

Lawrence "Larry" Ford, 72 years old, of Yuba City, California, died on August 14 at the Sunny View Adult Community Rest in that city.

He was born on April 14, 1890, to Josiah and Sarah Todd Ford at Hardenbergh, New York.

He was predeceased by his twin brother, Gerald "Jerry" Ford, in 1955.

He is survived by two sons, James Ford of Camden, New Jersey, and William Ford of State College, Pennsylvania; two daughters, Maria Ford Sprague of Grass Valley, California, and Carmen Ford of Steamboat Springs, Colorado; six grandchildren and two great-grandchildren.

Mr. Ford was a long-time resident of South Branch and was co- owner, with his brother, of Big Rock Farm of that place. On his brother's death, Mr. Ford succeeded to the full ownership of the farm although he no longer resided there.

Interment will be in the community cemetery at South Branch. Other funeral arrangements had not been completed at this writing.

Chapter 8

The End of the Rainbow

WARD HURRIED OUT THE BACK DOOR of the house and across to the two-car garage he had converted into an office when he retired from the State of New York. He switched on the light over the large drafting table where he had been plotting the deeds to the Ford farm and the properties adjoining it into a working base map. The deeds were scattered about the surface of the table along with a number of maps of earlier surveys that he had also been using to compile a composite map of the boundary lines, corners, and features of all the properties.

He finally found the deeds he was looking for. Back in 1955, Jerry Ford had given him the originals of the two deeds covering the farm when he first talked to Ward about surveying it. The first deed was the one from 1802 when Caleb Ford acquired the farm from Chauncey Musgrave. The second was dated in 1906 and quitclaimed the same parcel of land from Colonel Jonathan Craig, the then-owner of the remainder Musgrave lands, to Josiah Ford, Jerry's father. Ward had wondered about the later deed and Jerry said his mother had told him that his father had wanted to make sure he had no trouble with Craig as to where their common boundary line was although, as far as Jerry's mother knew, they had had no misunderstanding before. Both deeds were handwritten and it was the later one, which Jerry had told him was written by his father, in which Ward was the most interested. He compared the handwriting of this deed with the handwriting of the short note in the back of the book of Sherlock Holmes stories and, although he was certainly no authority, he was sure both writings were by the same hand. In particular, the "st" of step in the note was written exactly the same as the "st" in stone wall in the deed. Ward had no doubt that Josiah Ford had written both.

That confirmation was exciting enough, but Ward's hands trembled as he read the phrases in the two deeds describing the spring rights that ran as an appurtenance to the land. The 1802 deed stated:

"**Together with** one half of the water of the spring on lands of said party of the first part in back of the above lands and further up the mountain and the right to run the same to said lands."

That language was complete and expressed the intention of the two parties to the deed well enough, Ward thought; however, the 1906 deed went into some detail to accomplish the same thing.

"**Further** confirming the right of the party of the second part to take one half of the water from the Musgrave spring, so-called, situate on lands of the party of the first part aforesaid and the right to go upon said lands to locate, lay, maintain, repair, and replace a pipeline or some other device to carry such water beginning at said Musgrave spring and running north-easterly to and into lands of the party of the second part herein and as described hereinabove."

The need for the second deed hadn't seemed necessary to Ward all along. The description of the land didn't vary much from the first deed to the second, although the second deed did refine the bearings and distances stated. Otherwise, no real material change was made. The major difference was in the way the spring right was handled and, as Ward now noted, the word beginning in the second deed was underlined, which was unusual. It was almost as if the writer wanted to make it clear that something other than the spring run began there. Also, the name of the spring was cited twice. Ward had before pondered the need for the expanded language; now he thought he knew the reason for it.

As best Ward could remember, the only Sherlock Holmes story that used a step or a pace as a unit of measure was "The Musgrave Ritual." In this tale, a seemingly senseless ritual, consisting of a series of questions and answers, had been passed down through the Musgrave family for centuries. No one in the family knew the purpose or meaning of the ritual, but apparently in connection with it, the Musgrave family butler disappeared. Holmes, who was a college classmate of young Reginald Musgrave, was asked to look into the disappearance and, in his usual analytical fashion, solved that and the ritual at the same time. The first part of the ritual, with reference to an oak tree and an elm tree, determined the point of beginning. That was followed by a sequence of directions and distances with the distances being expressed, in each case, by a number of steps. Holmes worked out the point of beginning, paced out the directions, and found the butler's body at the end of the last course in a small cellar hidden under a large flagstone. The cellar also held a brass-bound box that contained the crown of Charles I of England and a number of coins dating from the time of his reign.

If Ward was right in his thinking, he had the point of beginning for the present ritual; it was the Musgrave spring. He leafed to the fifth story of the eleven that make up the collection entitled *The Memoirs of Sherlock Holmes* and scanned through the text of "The Musgrave Ritual." The words of the actual ritual are about half-way through the story and it was to this that Ward turned the pages.

The first lines referred to something apparently hidden. Once Holmes solved the riddle, he was able to fix the point of beginning by measurements of the length of the shadow cast by the elm tree. It was from this point that the courses were to be "stepped." The first of these went north "by ten and by ten," which meant (taking Holmes' solution) ten paces or steps with each foot or twenty single paces in all.

Ward moved the papers from the drafting table to clear the base map of the Ford property on which he had been working. All the boundary lines had been plotted and he had also been able to plot the location of the Musgrave spring by using the map he had made of his survey for the State purchase back in the 1920s. He laid out a due north line from the spring and, using the scale as set down by Josiah Ford in the back of the book, measured off twenty chains (1320 feet) along it. The next course in the ritual ran east for a distance of "by five and by five" or ten paces. Ward plotted a due east line with a length of ten chains (660 feet). The third course ran south "by two and by two," so Ward next plotted a due south line four chains (264 feet) long. The fourth and final course in the ritual called for running west "by one and by one." He plotted this course due west for two chains (132 feet).

All this rather complicated the issue. Nothing that the first course ran north for twenty chains and the third course ran south for four chains, Ward subtracted the third distance from the first, which left a north of only sixteen chains (1056 feet). Similarly, the second course ran east for ten chains and the fourth course ran west for two chains. Ward subtracted the fourth distance from the second leaving an east course of eight chains (528 feet). This left a right triangle with a base (the line running east and west) of eight chains and a side of sixteen chains. Ward then computed the length of the hypotenuse (the side of the triangle opposite the right angle) by the Pythagorean theorum — i.e., the square on the hypotenuse is equal to the sum of the squares on the other two sides — and arrived at a length of 17.889 chains (1180.64 feet). He next computed the bearing of the hypotenuse by the tangent function (Tangent angle A = side opposite divided by the side adjacent) to determine that it ran North 26 degrees 33 minutes 50 seconds East. However, if, as he assumed, the scale was inscribed in the book at the time of the later deed to the Ford farm, then this was the date the ritual had been laid out on the ground by Josiah Ford. Therefore, Ward had to apply the secular change of magnetic declination that had occurred between then,

1906, and the present. Referring to the U. S. Coast and Geodetic Survey tables, he found this to be a minus change of 2 degrees 07 minutes. Applying this factor to his computed bearing, Ward arrived at North 24 degrees 26 minutes 50 seconds East as the magnetic bearing of the line he would have to run from the Musgrave spring, the point of beginning of Josiah Ford's ritual.

The plotting Ward now had on his base map fit the call in the 1906 deed as "beginning at said Musgrave spring and running northeasterly to and into lands of the party of the second part. . . ." Although he had never located the big rock by survey, from his knowledge of where it lay on the ground in relation to the boundary lines of the Ford farm, he was sure it was very near the terminus of the hypotenuse line as he had it plotted.

Betty returned home from her sewing club while Ward was in the midst of his computation and mapping. She looked in at the office door and asked how much longer he planned to work. He told her not to wait up for him as he would be a while yet. He decided not to tell her of his suppositions until he was sure he really had made a discovery.

Ward slept little that night and was again up before the sun. He put up a sandwich and an apple, filled his water jugs, and carried them all out to the office where he added them to the rucksack he had packed the night before. It included a steel chain tape, his hand compass, and a set of chaining pins, something he had not used for some time. This consisted of eleven metal pins, about the diameter of a pencil and about eight inches long, with a point on one end and a loop on the other end. Each pin looked like a miniature eye bolt. The pins were carried on a large steel ring that snapped open so the loops of the pins could be slipped on, much like a ring of keys. The set was completed by an empty second ring, the same size and style as the first.

Ward drove Route 42 to the Deep Notch and parked his car at the pull-out just over the top. He had decided to walk to the spring over the State lands rather than up from the Ford farm buildings so he wouldn't have to go through a series of explanations in case he ran into Bill or Maria. He toiled up the slope; it was much steeper from this direction, but he took few rests, so anxious was he to test his theory. Finally, he reached the spring and here took a long sit-down on a rock beside it. The Musgrave spring was dry now, but one time it had flowed a steady stream of cold, clear, pure water.

Ward uncoiled the one-chain tape, laying it flat along the ground as he handed off each separate loop behind him while he walked along. The evening before he had set the North 24 degrees 26 minutes 50 seconds East bearing on his hand compass, but checked it again. Actually, the hand compass couldn't be set that fine; his setting was as close to North 24 degrees 30 minutes East as he could make it. He took one of the chaining pins off the filled ring, put it through the small metal ring at one end of the chain, and stuck it in the ground at the lip of the spring. He took a sight along the bearing on the compass and walked down it pulling the chain behind him. When the chain came up tight against the pin anchoring it, Ward made sure it lay straight and flat against the ground. He then took a second pin and put it through the small ring on that end of the chain, pinning it to the ground. He walked back up the hill, pulled the first pin from the ground at the lip of the spring and put it on the empty one of the two large rings. Of course, to get a true measurement of distance, it should have been taken level and not along the ground as he was doing, but Ward felt that Josiah or whomever had originally laid out this line (if, indeed, it ever had been laid out), would have done it by measuring along the ground, that being about the only way one person could measure with a tape. It took two people to get any accuracy on a level measurement, and Ward was quite sure Josiah Ford would have set this ritual alone.

At the end of ten chains, which Ward knew he had reached because the second ring now held ten of the chaining pins and the first ring was empty. The eleventh pin was stuck in the ground at the lower end of the chain. Here Ward was in a small grove of hemlock trees, remnants left by the tanners back in the 1800s, when they had cleared most of the hemlock from the Catskill Mountains. He noticed some marks on one of the trees about fifteen feet to his right and slightly downhill from where he stood. He walked toward it and felt his heart beat faster as he saw the figure "10" scribed into the bark of the tree. He could estimate the age of the scribing from the appearance of it and made it to be about 50 or 60 years old. He knew then he was on the right track and felt sure that "track" had been left by Josiah Ford. He also knew by the lay of the land that the bearing he was on was going to take him near the big rock.

Ward moved over to the scribed tree and took his next sight of the bearing from it. He also began his next measurement from the tree so as to get his line to agree more closely with the one that had been originally laid out. At the end of the fifteenth chain, he could see the big rock looming up through the trees ahead. When he reached the distance of 17.889 chains, he was still some fifty feet short of the rock and a little to the west of it. Just left of where he put a chaining pin in the ground to mark the terminus of the course he had run was a large rock. It was one of those that had slid down the slope in the distant past. A pile of earth was in front of it on the downhill side where it had been pushed up during the slide. The two sides of the rock were also partly covered. However, the back or upper side of the rock was somewhat exposed by the gully created by the slide.

Ward hadn't known just what he would find at the end of the distance and bearing, but he had brought along a surplus U. S. Army entrenching tool he had bought somewhere, but had hardly ever used. The words of the Musgrave ritual following the four directional courses were "and so under," so Ward knew he was going to have to dig under something. He decided now that it must be the rock.

Ward got down on his knees on the upper side of the rock and started digging away at the ground there. It was all covered by leaves, twigs, and old limbs and was grown over by a blackberry bush. He moved this all out of the way and dug into the dirt behind it. At a depth of about a foot, he exposed a small wall made of flat stones, obviously laid up by human hands. He pulled these out one by one and saw that the wall covered the opening of a small cavern reaching under the bottom of the rock. Something was in there, but he couldn't quite make it out in the darkness. He reached in and felt a handle on the object. He pulled on it and slid out into the open a chest about two feet by two feet and a foot deep.

The chest was entirely covered with brass to protect it from the weather and animals and the effects of being buried. A broken padlock hung from the hasp on the front of the chest. Although Ward had seen the key on the rock where it had lain as one of the effects in Jerry Ford's pocket for only a few seconds, he was sure it was of a style that would fit this lock. The padlock was, however, so rusted the key wouldn't have worked, so it had been broken to open the chest.

Ward put on the pair of gloves he had brought along, removed the padlock, and opened the chest. The inside of it was lined with zinc to provide added protection against damage from water and dampness to anything that had been kept there. A hammer lay on top of the items in the chest. It was the same kind of hammer that was missing from the Ford farm workshop. Ward noted the dark brownish stains on the head of it and concluded that it had, indeed, been the murder weapon.

The hammer lay on top of an old rucksack that rattled and clanked when Ward picked it up. Opening it, he found it held a number of metal wedges just like those Carmen had described to him as having been made by her Uncle Jerry and used by the two of them to climb the big rock. Ward took one of the wedges and walked over to the side of the big rock. Looking carefully at the surface of it beneath where he knew the eyebolt to be, he saw a series of horizontal cracks. Peering more closely, he saw where the rock surface seemed to be scratched or chipped around some of the cracks. He took the wedge and found that it slid easily into one of them to a depth of about one inch. A few whacks with the hammer and it would be solid, he thought.

He returned to the chest. Under the rucksack was a coil of rope. As he took it out of the chest, he estimated the length of it to be about sixty feet or just long enough so that when it was threaded through the eyebolt, the double strand of it would reach the ground on the upper side of the big rock. The rope was, however, only a minor thing compared to the two items that lay in the bottom of the chest.

One of these was a hand compass Ward recognized as his own. It was the one he had lent to Jerry Ford back in 1955 when he said he wanted to check some lines of the land of the farm that was going to then be subdivided into the shares of his and Larry's separate ownerships. Ward had forgotten all about the compass.

He had also forgotten about the one-chain tape he had lent to Jerry at the same time. There it lay in the bottom of the chest. It was done up in perfect loops, laid one over the other. The long leather thongs on each end of the tape were wrapped around and around the layers of the chain and the ends of them were tied together in a neat bow. Ward knew only one person who added that finishing touch when doing up a tape.

The Windham Journal
Windham, New York
Thursday, August 23, 1962

n.b. The following article comes to *The Windham Journal* courtesy of the *Yuba City News*, Yuba City, California, where it first appeared in the August 17, 1962, issue of that newspaper.

Body of Missing Woman Found

The body of Maria Sprague, who was reported missing on August 14, was found today. A fisherman on the Middle Fork of the Yuba River found the body of Sprague still in her car, a 1960 Chevrolet two-door sedan, where it had evidently come to rest after leaving Route 20. The car was partly in the stream opposite a sharp curve and beneath a steep ledge of rocks bordering the highway. The find was made at about 11:00 AM and the name of the fisherman was not released.

Rob Pratt, Sheriff of Yuba County, in an interview with this paper, stated that Sprague was reported missing on the evening of Tuesday, August 14, after leaving her home in Grass Valley earlier in the day. A friend of Sprague's, who had been with her that morning, told Sheriff Pratt that Sprague had received a telephone call from the Sunny View Adult Community Rest Home that her father, Lawrence Ford, who was a resident there, was declining and had asked that she be called to come to his bedside. The friend had reported, said Sheriff Pratt, that Sprague was very upset on receiving the call and had left the house immediately. Sprague never arrived at the rest home and Lawrence Ford passed away later that same morning.

Sheriff Pratt told this newspaper that the Sprague car left the highway at a sharp turn near Browns Valley, about halfway between Grass Valley and Yuba City, and had tumbled over the steep embankment to come to rest at the edge of the stream. No skid marks were found at the scene and Sheriff Pratt concluded that Sprague may have been traveling at an imprudent rate of speed and lost control of the car. No flat tires or mechanical defects were found on the car.

The coroner of Yuba County, in his report, stated that death was caused by multiple internal injuries resulting from the crash and was instantaneous. The instant of death was set at 11:32 AM, the time shown on both the clock, which was smashed on impact, in the Sprague car and the wrist watch that Sprague was wearing, which was also broken and had stopped at the same time. A check of the death certificate for Lawrence Ford shows that his death occurred at 11:43 AM, just minutes after the death of his daughter, who was enroute to be at his side.

It is reported that Sprague will be interred in the family cemetery plot at her childhood home in New York State. Sprague is survived by twin sons, Jeremiah and Jeffrey, who are serving their internship at Good Samaritan Hospital in Sacramento.

Chapter 9

Confession

WARD EASTMAN SAT ON THE GROUND beside the now-empty chest, stunned at the things scattered about him. He had thought, after his discovery of the notation in the book the evening before, that today he would find something, would find solutions to some of the puzzles that perplexed him. And he had. But some of the answers, now he had them, made him sad, made him wish he hadn't gotten himself involved to the extent that he was. But these answers only posed more questions.

He had found the location of the Ford family treasure; but what was it? He had found the murder weapon and he knew who had used it; but why had she? If the chest had really held a treasure; where was it? The most disturbing question of all was: What was Ward himself going to do now that he alone (other than the murderer herself, of course) had all this information?

The immediate answer was to put everything back and talk to Maria before doing anything else. Ward replaced the items back in the chest as he had found them; the chain, so carefully done up and so telling, went in the bottom. He placed the compass within the coils of it, but not before he snapped it open to see what bearing was set on it. It was North 24 degrees 30 minutes East: so Jerry Ford had run through the same computation as he had. He placed the coil of rope next and the rucksack, with the wedges inside it, on top of that. He laid the hammer in last, closed the chest, snapped the hasp shut, and hooked the broken padlock through it. He slid the chest under the sloping bottom of the rock and pushed it back to the position where it had been before. He collected together the flat stones and laid them up into a miniature wall across the front of the opening under the rock. He shoveled the dirt back into place against the wall being sure not to leave any traces of loose dirt scattered on the ground where he had first shoveled it. He even reset the blackberry bush and tamped it firmly in place. He randomly replaced the loose leaves, twigs, and dead sticks over it all. When he was done, it was difficult to tell that any disturbance had taken place.

He walked slowly down the mountain slope into the Deep Notch dreading the confrontation he knew must take place. When he drove into the parking area in back of the Ford farmhouse, he saw Maria was again puttering in the wildflower garden that grew there. She stood up when she saw him and mopped her brow with the back of her hand leaving a smudge of dirt across it.

"Hi. I didn't expect you back so soon. Come on into the kitchen and sit down; I've left all the windows open and a cool breeze is blowing through. I've just made a fresh pitcher of lemonade; have a glass with me — these July days are hot. Bill's gone to Catskill for something and I've been hoping someone would drop by. Have you had your lunch? I can make you a sandwich."

Ward mumbled that he had eaten his lunch, which he hadn't. He had forgotten all about eating even though he had packed the lunch that morning. He had carried it in his rucksack up the mountain and down again and it was still there, now in the trunk of the car. He followed Maria into the kitchen and sat down at the table. She poured him a glass of lemonade and one for herself. The ice cubes tinkled in the tall glasses. He waited until she sat in the chair opposite him.

"I found the chest under the rock."

Maria sat silently, not moving, for a few minutes. The expression on her face didn't change, but Ward noticed a sadness deep in her eyes. "I knew someday someone would find it," she finally said. "I guess I thought all along you'd be the one."

"Do you want to talk about what happened? I've told no one what I've found and I put everything back just the way it was. I decided to hear your story before doing anything further."

"I don't think a day has gone by that I haven't thought at least once about what I did and cursed myself for it. On the other hand, I didn't do anything about it and left Uncle Jerry up there all these years. In a way, that's worse than the day itself. It's a long story. It needs to be told. I've wanted to tell it before, but didn't. I guess it's time I did.

"I didn't know where Uncle Jerry was that morning anymore than anyone else did. We talked about it; we all wondered, but we did up his chores and, one by one, each went off on his own. Then I realized that I was the only one left. I made up my mind that I'd go somewhere too, so I packed a small lunch and rode off on the last motor scooter still there.

"Back when I was growing up, I had a favorite hike I went on whenever I wanted to be alone. I would ride my bicycle down to the village and then up the road to the bottom of Deep Notch. I always had to walk my bike up there; it was too steep and too long for me to ride. Bill was the only one I ever knew who could ride all the way to the top. But once I got there, I could coast down the other side and that made the hard work of walking up all worthwhile. At the bottom of the Notch, a woods road cuts off the main road and runs easterly into the old Craig property. I think it was a logging road once. I could ride up that quite a ways. When I got to the steep part, I'd hide the bike behind some brush and hike up the mountain, which is the one right here in back of the farm. When I got to the top, I'd come down this side to the old spring and then follow the waterline down to the house. In the evening, Uncle Jerry would drive me around in his truck and we'd pick up my bike and bring it home.

"So this day I decided to take that hike one more time. I wondered if I could still find my way; it had been years since I'd done it last. This time was a lot easier and faster because I had the motor scooter. When I got to the end of the woods road, I found Uncle Jerry's truck parked there. I wondered why, but really didn't think much more about it. I opened the tail gate and laid one of those old boards he always carried around in the back of the truck against it. I wheeled the motor scooter up that ramp and put it in the back of the truck. I put the board back and closed the tail gate. I wrote a note to Uncle Jerry and stuck it under the windshield wiper so he'd be sure to see it. I told him the scooter was mine and to take it home when he went because I was walking over the mountain just like I used to when I was a kid.

"The mountain seemed a lot higher than it was in my younger days, but I made good time and found my way easily to the top. I didn't have any trouble locating the spring either, although it had gone dry some years before. Instead of following the old waterline, I decided to go somewhere near the big rock where I could sit on top of the ledge and enjoy the view while I ate an early lunch.

"When I got near the big rock, I saw someone was sitting on top of it. When I realized it was Uncle Jerry, I hollared to him. He seemed startled when he looked up, but when he saw it was me he said for me to come over because he had something I should see. As I got closer, I saw a chain tape laying on the ground and what looked like an old iron chest sitting beside a hole that had been dug under a rock. Uncle Jerry's rucksack and a shovel lay nearby.

"I asked him how I was supposed to get up the rock to where he was and he told me to go over to where the rope hung down the face of it. When I got there, he leaned over the edge of the rock and told me to hang on the rope while he pulled it up. I was to put my feet on the metal wedges that stuck out of the rock and climb up them like a ladder. I was scared at first, but it turned out to be a safe and easy climb, with Uncle Jerry protecting my every move.

"What he wanted to show me was this old album. It was a fancy thing, all bound in leather; it looked like it had been special made. It was a stamp album, page after page of stamps. Some pages held only one stamp. Neither Uncle Jerry nor I knew much about stamps, but we knew enough to realize that the album must be worth a lot of money. If nothing else, it was old he told me because every stamp in it was from before 1905. I asked him why he was so sure of that and he said because that's when it had been stolen. Then he told me how he knew that was so."

" 'Most people around here think I've spent all my life on this farm. I guess that's mostly because they're all too young to remember that your dad and I didn't come here until we were about ten years old. My father was gamekeeper on this large estate in the back end of Ulster County. That's where he met my mother and that's where Larry and I were born. When my grandfather died in 1900, my grandmother couldn't run the farm by herself, so she asked my father to come back here and take over the property for her. He didn't want to, but the man who owned the estate where he worked and where he lived insisted that my father had an obligation to his mother and pretty much made him come. My father resented that, but I didn't realize how much.

" 'Well, we settled down here; that is, my mother, Larry and I did. My father was always a restless sort and really wasn't very interested in being a farmer. My mother kept at him to pay more attention to the needs of the farm, but he kept saying, "Oh, don't worry about it. Someday we'll find a treasure big enough so none of us will ever have to work again. Just be patient until our ship comes in.

" 'The ship never did come in and we never did find any treasure. Then, in the spring of 1906, my father got swept downstream in a flood; we found his body down below Lexington. I didn't give much more thought to the treasure or our overdue ship, although my mother insisted right up until the day she died that it was out there, just waiting to dock because my father had told her so. After she died, I kind of forgot about the whole thing.

" 'Then, a couple of years ago, I found this key in the library, hidden in a place where only my father could have put it. When I couldn't find any lock that it fit, I made up my mind that maybe a family tresure did exist somewhere, only I didn't know where or what it was. I got the idea my father must have left some clue that would direct me to the location of it and that most likely it was in one of his books in the library. Since then, I've spent a lot of time going through book after book with no luck until last night when you were at the movies. At first, I couldn't figure out all of what the clue meant, but then I remembered some crazy wording in a deed to the farm — a deed my father had written himself the winter before he died. I had given the original deed to Ward Eastman to help when he surveyed the property, but I had written out a copy, which I kept. When I put the two things together – the deed and the clue I found – I figured out where to go. And here we are and here's the family treasure after all these years.'

"With that, Uncle Jerry held out the album. It was then I saw the name 'Samuel C. Huntington' inscribed in gold on the cover."

" 'That name may not mean anything to you,' Uncle Jerry continued, 'but that's the name of the man who owned the property where my father worked when Larry and I were little. When I found it just a few minutes ago everything made sense. In that same winter before my father died, the caretaker of the Huntington estate was found murdered. His body was in the main lodge and the speculation was that he had caught a burglar or a housebreaker in the building and that person had shot him. I can remember my father and mother talking about it because they both knew and liked the caretaker when they lived at the estate. I remember him too; he was a nice man and was very kind and pleasant to Larry and me.

" 'Nothing was ever said about what, if anything, had been stolen and the murderer was never caught. Now I know what was stolen – this stamp album – and who the murderer was. It was my father. He was a great bear hunter; he used to roam all over the mountains, especially in the fall and early winter. Sometimes he would be gone for days at a time. It would have been no mean feat for him to walk over the hills from here to the Huntington property. And he would have known all about this stamp album, where it was kept, and how much it was worth. He must have hidden it here that spring just before he died with the idea that in a few years, after the news of the murder had faded away, he would start selling the stamps, one by one, for a continuing source of cash. But he died long before that time came.'

"I was absolutely astounded by the whole story. My grandfather a murderer; I could hardly believe it. But then I realized just what we had. If the stamps in that album were valuable in 1905, think what they would be worth fifty years later. 'What are you going to do with the album now?' I asked him."

" 'I'm going to see that it gets back to the Huntington family.'

" 'But if you do that, you'll have to tell how you got it and then everyone will know who committed the murder back when it was stolen. You can't do that; think how all the kids will feel about people knowing their great-grandfather was a murderer.'

" 'I suppose so, but it's the right thing to do and I have to do it that way.'

" 'But no one probably even remembers about the stamp album anyway. The Huntingtons have got so much money they don't need this added to it. I think we should keep it, sell the stamps, and split the money between you and my father, me and my brothers and sister. We could all use it. Especially my father; then I wouldn't have to support him. And my boys want to go to medical school. This would pay their way through; I don't know how I can send them otherwise.'

" 'That would be as bad as stealing it in the first place. You're beginning to sound as bad as my father. I always tried to teach you right from wrong, but I guess I failed.'

"That only made me madder. All I could think about was here was the answer to all my prayers. Here was all the money I would ever need to take care of my sons and enough so that my father could take care of himself. After the way he had treated me and with what my husband had done to me, I deserved better. I guess I lost my head. I picked up the hammer that lay there on the top of the rock. 'You can't do that Uncle Jerry. You can't do that,' I said, and swung the hammer at him. I hit him in the head. He tried to back up, but I just kept hitting him. He fell backward with blood running down his face and lay still there on the big rock. I realized then what I had done. He was dead; he didn't move; I sat down and cried.

"After awhile I got myself together. I knew I couldn't change what I had done and decided I might just as well make the best of it. I put the album back in some rubberized canvas it had been wrapped in, tied one end of the rope around it, and let it down to the ground. I climbed down the wedges in the side of the rock while hanging on the rope; I had tied the other end of it to an eyebolt that was sticking out of the top of the rock. I untied the album and left it laying there while I climbed back up the rock. I untied the rope and threaded it through the eyebolt so that two strands of it hung over the edge. I climbed back down the wedges and knocked each one out with the hammer after I stepped down to the one below it. When I reached the ground, I pulled the rope down after me. I did up the chain tape that was laying there and put it and a hand compass that was with it into the chest. I coiled up the rope, put the wedges in Uncle Jerry's old rucksack,and put all that, together with the hammer, into the chest, closed it and put a broken padlock that also lay there through the hasp.

"I could see where the chest had been under a rock, so I slid it back there as far as I could push it. A number of flat stones were laying beside the rock and I built these up into a little wall across the front of the hole. A shovel also laid there and I used it to pile all the loose dirt over the wall. Then I took a lot of dead leaves and loose twigs and scattered those over the dirt. When I got done, everything looked like it naturally belonged there. I took the album and shovel and climbed back up the mountain and over the top. Somewhere along the way, I hid the shovel under an old dead tree that was flat on the ground.

"When I got to the truck, everything was just like I had left it; my note was still stuck under the windshield wiper, so I was pretty sure no one else had been there. I had taken the keys to the truck from Uncle Jerry's pocket, so I got in and drove it back down the hollow. I took Route 28 to Kingston, then Route 9W to Catskill, went over the Rip Van Winkle Bridge to Hudson, and left the truck in the parking lot at the train station. Not far from the station, I saw a small wooded area with a pull-off into it. I drove in there, unloaded the motor scooter, and secured it to a tree with the lock and chain that came with it. After parking the truck in the station parking lot, I walked back to where the scooter was and rode away on it. I threw the truck keys into the Hudson River when I went back across the bridge. I went from Catskill to Durham, up Mt. Pisgah, over North Settlement and Jewett Heights, and through Lexington back to South Branch.

"I took the stamp album home to California and put it in a safe deposit box in the bank. Every time I needed some money for college tuition or something, I sold some of the stamps — not the real rare ones — to this dealer in San Francisco. The album still has a lot of stamps in it and it's still in that same safe deposit box. I suppose I'll have to do something with it now. I guess I'm really not much different than my grandfather. We each murdered a good friend and we each were going to profit from something that wasn't ours. Only he didn't live long enough to be as bad as I am.

"The worst thing is, not only will I loose the money from the stamps, I'll lose my share of the sale of the farm. Somewhere I read that a murderer can't profit from the act of the murder. That means that when my father dies, I can't inherit what came to him because of Uncle Jerry's death. Of course, if I died first, then my inheritance would go directly to my sons because that's the way my father's will is written. That's all unlikely because my father isn't going to live much longer now. He was getting more feeble day by day just before I left to come east.

"Can I make a bargain with you? I'm leaving day after tomorrow to go home. I'll send the stamp album to you so that you can return it to the Huntington family. Don't say anything about what you know or found until after my father dies, which will probably be only a matter of a few weeks. Then, when I come back here for his funeral — he wants to be buried here at South Branch — I'll go with you to the police and tell them what I've told you today."

Ward agreed to Maria's request; it really seemed to him that a few more weeks after all these years wouldn't make much difference. And he felt he should give her the chance to talk to her sons before they read the whole story in the newspapers. Only things didn't turn out that way. The album did come in the mail a few days after Maria had returned home. Larry Ford did die in a few weeks. But so did Maria and, coincidently (or not), just before her father's death. So her share of the proceeds from the sale of the farm would devolve directly to her sons after all. The funeral for Larry Ford was a double funeral. When Maria's body was found, the family asked the undertaker to hold Larry's body for a few more days so that he and Maria could be buried together in the family plot in the cemetery on the bluff in back of South Branch.

Ward was a bearer at the funeral and, as he stood in the cemetery at the graveside service, he looked around at the grieving family (they were all back in South Branch again) and wondered if it was really necessary that they—or anyone else—know their family tree had a murderer or two amongst the branches.

Catskill Mountain News
Margaretville, New York
Thursday, September 13, 1962

Long-Lost Family Heirloom Returned — Mystery Deepens

In an interview with this newspaper, Gordon Huntington confirmed that a valuable stamp album, which had been stolen from the family lodge at Hardenbergh over fifty years ago, was returned to the family by mail. Huntington said the album was a stamp collection put together by his great-grandfather, Samuel C. Huntington, over the latter part of the 1800s. His great-grandfather had started the collection when he was a boy and had continued to add to it up to the time it was stolen, Huntington said. The family had long ago given up the album as being gone forever and some of the younger generation weren't even aware that it existed. The family was, therefore, totally surprised when the package arrived in the mail and, on opening it, to find the album. Huntington said that no letter, note, or other writing was included with the package, but that he had immediately called the State Police to notify them of the incident.

The album together with the wrappings from it were turned over to BCI Investigator Wendell Avery of the local State Police barracks. Avery told this newspaper that the investigation was continuing, but no leads had been uncovered. The album had been wrapped for mailing in regular kraft paper and tied with twine, both of which items were very common and could be purchased in any department store, Avery said. The address and return address had both been printed in ink with the return addressee being J. Hotaling, 136 Forest Street, Brattleboro, Vermont. Avery said he had contacted the sheriff of Windham County in Vermont and asked him to check on that name and address. The report back said that no such address existed in Brattleboro and that neither did any Hotaling with a first initial "J" or otherwise.

Investigator Avery further disclosed that the postmark on the package showed that it had been mailed from Stockbridge, Massachusetts, on Saturday, September 1. Avery stated that he had driven to Stockbridge, and in company with the sheriff of Berkshire County, had questioned the postmaster there. The postmaster had no recollection of the package or of the person who mailed it pointing out, Avery said, that Saturday had been on the Labor Day holiday weekend and the village of Stockbridge and the post office were crowded with tourists. While in Stockbridge, Avery had checked for the address and name that had been given as the return address on the package, but nothing came of these inquiries.

Gordon Huntington noted that some of the stamps originally in the album are missing. The more valuable stamps have not been disturbed, Huntington reported, but a number of the others, less valuable, but still of considerable worth these nearly sixty years later, had been removed.

A review of early issues of this newspaper discloses that the album was stolen from the Huntington lodge on December 10, 1905. In connection with the theft, the caretaker of the Huntington estate in Hardenbergh, one Michael "Mike" Fairbairn, was shot to death. The body of Fairbairn was found by his wife on the floor of the library in the lodge. She had gone looking for her husband when he didn't return from his daily inspection of the lodge, which was closed for the winter. Apparently Fairbairn had surprised an intruder in the library and had been shot while trying to apprehend him. The police were called in immediately, but as a heavy snow had been falling most of the day, they were unable to find any tracks leading to or from the lodge. An inventory of the library was made at the time and it was found that only the stamp album was missing.

Later issues of the newspaper reported the usual "continuing investigations," but the murderer was never identified. In time, the story faded and nothing more was heard about it until the return of the stamp album a week ago.

Chapter 10

Retrospective

THE SATURDAY of the Labor Day weekend was warm and sunny, just the right kind of day to close out the summer season. Ward Eastman left early that morning on his drive to Stockbridge. He told Betty he was off to look over a survey, but she was uninterested. This was the first day of the three-day fair down on the church lawn and she was in charge of the table displaying all the quilts, aprons, and other articles that had been made by her sewing circle over the past year.

The drive took over two hours, because the highways were filled with travelers hurrying here and there trying to get the most out of this last holiday of the summer. However crowded the highway was, it was nothing compared to what greeted him when he turned the corner at the Red Lion Inn and looked down the main street of Stockbridge. The sidewalks on both sides of the street were packed with people and every parking space along the way was filled. He finally found a spot some distance from the post office and walked back to it, his package under his arm.

The stamp album had come to Ward in the mail shortly after Maria arrived back in California, just as she had promised. It was a beautiful volume, especially considering all the years it had been buried under the rock. However, the brass-covered chest had been well-built and had protected its contents from its surroundings, the weather, and any creeping or crawling things that might have entered the small cavern where it lay hidden. And the canvas covering in which the album had been securely wrapped had kept it dry all those years.

In his youth, Ward had been a minor stamp collector, just like all boys, he supposed. His collection hadn't really amounted to much and he had never taken it up again after his small album had burned in the fire that claimed the lives of his mother and father. Still, he remembered a bit about stamps and always wondered just what a major collection would hold. He was not disappointed when he opened the Huntington volume.

As Maria had told him, some pages in the album held only one stamp. On the very first display page was a British Guiana 1856 1 c Magenta. His recollection was that only one of these existed in the world or maybe his memory was faulty because here was another one. The next page held an 1851 British Guiana cover with two 2 c circular stamps. Ward had never heard of these before. Following that was a page holding another single stamp – this one the Penny Black, the 1840 Great Britain stamp containing a portrait of Queen Victoria. This one, Ward remembered, had been the first adhesive postage stamp. On and on it went, stamps from Mauritius, Sweden, Nova Scotia, Hawaii, and all around the world, places he supposed had been visited by Samuel Huntington over the years he put this collection together.

But the album had to be returned to its rightful owner. Ward knew that. Still, he could enjoy for a little time experiencing a collection such as he would never see again. Finally, he closed the album and wrapped it carefully in the heavy paper he had purchased at the S. S. Kresge store in Kingston the last time he had been to the County Clerk's Office there. He tied it tightly with some twine he had bought at the same place and then printed the Huntington's address on the outside. He thought a minute or two about not putting down any return address, but concluded the postmaster might ask about it and that would call attention to himself and the package, which he didn't want. So he dreamed one up out of thin air and added it to the package.

The walk back to the Stockbridge Post Office was spent dodging people going this way and that. Ward didn't think he looked as "touristy" as most of them, but still he blended in with the crowd. The post office too was filled with tourists sending out post cards to Aunt Ellen and Uncle Joe saying, "Wish you were here," and not meaning it. He was thankful for the bustle – the postmaster hardly looked up as he accepted the package, weighed it, and made change from Ward's five-dollar bill.

On the journey back home, Ward took a roundabout route, passing through East Jewett, the place of his youth, and stopped at the little cemetery there. He sat on the low stone wall bordering the cemetery and next to the graves of his mother and father. He lit up his pipe, looked at the mountains ringing the valley, mountains he had first climbed with his father, and thought back to a time long ago.

Ward had not been surprised when he unwrapped the package that came from Maria. He knew just what the stamp album would look like – he had seen it before. It was just before Christmas in what he now knew was 1905. He had been five years old then and it was the first Christmas that really meant anything to him. He couldn't sleep nights wondering what present he would get from his mother and father. He wanted so many things — he knew he wouldn't get them all. Yet he was sure that whatever it was, it would be special and something just for him. Just like all little boys do before Christmas, he looked in closets, under beds, and in other good hiding places around the house when his mother was at school and his father was outside. He wanted to see what size and shape his present was. Finally he found it or, at least, he thought he had.

His father's old rucksack hung as it always did on a nail in the wall of the shed that was built on the back of the house. One day, just a few days after his father had returned from a bear hunt, Ward noticed that the rucksack had something in it, something different from what it usually held. This seemed to be a square thing, like a box of some kind. However, Ward was too small to reach the rucksack and couldn't move anything to climb up on so he could look into it without his father realizing what he was doing. He was sure it was his present. However, as it turned out, it wasn't.

One day, only a couple of days before Christmas, he was in the kitchen. The door to the shed was partly open and he heard his father talking to someone. Ward looked through the crack in the doorjamb and saw that it was the man his father sometimes went hunting with. He couldn't hear what they talking about, but soon his father reached up for the rucksack and took it down. He opened it and took out the square thing that was in it and laid it on the work bench. He and the other man unwrapped the newspapers that were around it. It was a big book, Ward saw, and had a pretty leather cover. Something was written in gold letters across the front of it, but Ward couldn't see what it said and, even if he could, the words probably wouldn't have meant anything to him. His father and the other man turned through the pages of the book and Ward could see what looked like stamps and envelopes. Finally, the two men again wrapped the book in the newspapers and his father handed it to the other man, who put it into his own rucksack and went out the back door into the snow. Ward scurried into the front room before his father came into the kitchen. He'd just have to keep looking for his present, he thought, and wondered just where it could be hidden.

That had been a great number of Christmases ago and Ward didn't remember now what his present had been that year. His revery over, he realized it was getting late. He tapped out the cold ashes from his pipe on the stone wall. All that was in the past he decided and was best left there; he told his father so as he looked down at his grave. He walked out of the cemetery back to his car.

Ward felt unburdened as he drove home. He had found all the answers, the loose ends had all been tied together although he wished now some hadn't. With all that damn detective stuff out of the way, he'd have to start paying more attention to the business of land surveying. He'd get started on that tomorrow. It was the first of the month, and time to send out the bills to those who still owed him money for work he'd finished. He glanced at his watch as he drove through the Deep Notch.

"Damnation," he cursed out loud, "the post office just closed and it will be for the rest of this long weekend and I forgot to buy any stamps."

Author's Note

As the subtitle to this book suggests, it is a mix of fact and fancy. In some instances, the distinction between the two is obvious and one is easily separable from the other. The first three chapters—"The Hardenburgh Patent," "The Livingstons," and "The Early Surveyors"—are factual (except for the last paragraph in the third chapter) and are condensed from a much longer work entitled *The Hardenburgh Patent: The Largest Colonial Grant* now available through the New York State Association of Professional Land Surveyors. Similarly, the references to various writings by Sir Arthur Conan Doyle are correct, with the information about the first editions of some of them being taken from Ronald Burt DeWall's *The World Bibliography of Sherlock Holmes and Dr. Watson* (Bramhall House, New York, 1974).

Other factual passages are more subtle. The description of Ward Eastman's career with the State of New York is real, but Eastman himself is not. Some of the anecdotes about events involving various people are based on fact and others are not. The story of Brazil Pelham and *The Windham Journal* was told to me (more than once) many years ago by my uncle. He always maintained it was a true story, but I have my doubts and think it's more apocryphal than not.

Most of the place names—villages, towns, valleys, mountains, streams, highways, etc.—are real and are oriented one to another just the way they are on the ground. However, some locales have been fictionalized to better fit the story line.

Finally, none of the people in this book are real except for those noted above who include, of course, Sherlock Holmes and Dr. Watson. However, many of the characters are composites of the personalities, traits, and idiosyncrasies of individuals who do or did actually live in these Catskill Mountains.

October 22, 1991
Norman J. Van Valkenburgh
Kingston, New York

109

Norman J. Van Valkenburgh was born in West Kill in Greene County and has spent most of his life in or in sight of the Catskill Mountains. He is a licensed surveyor and 32-year veteran of the New York State Department of Environmental Conservation. He has written extensively about the Catskills and Adirondacks and is now associated with the firm of West and Brooks in Phoenicia, New York.

Purple Mountain Press is a publishing company committed to producing the best original books of regional interest as well as bringing back into print significant older works. In 1991 Purple Mountain Press published Norman Van Valkenburgh's *On the Adirondack Survey with Verplanck Colvin: The Diaries of Percy Reese Morgan*. For information about this title and other hard-to-find books about New York State, write: Purple Mountain Press, Ltd., Main St., P.O. Box E3, Fleischmanns, NY 12430 or call: 800-325-2665.